CW00869409

Maffee

and the

Space Detective

By

Xerxes E Setna

Table of Contents

Chapter One

Maffee was humming a tune to himself as he dusted the desktops. He tutted as he lifted up the brown coffee mug and saw the ring it had left on the shiny, silver desk. He pointed his right index finger at the stain and a jet of furniture polish sprayed out, which he then wiped thoroughly.

Maffee was a robot. A Mechanical Android Feature Five Eight Extended to be precise, or MAFFEE for short. He was tall and very slim, with a metallic pale blue exterior, the same as all MAFFEEs that were built in the year 2267.

However, Maffee was different from all the others. The fact that he spent his days cleaning, cooking, ironing and performing various other household duties made him very, very different. MAFFEEs were not created as domestic robots. They had been created as state-of-the-art designers of ultra-modern weapons for the InterEarth government and were more intelligent than any other robot or computer that had ever been produced.

Maffee had been assigned to the Secret Weapons Operational Research and Development team of the InterEarth government. The SWORD team, as it was called, designed the very latest and most advanced weapons on Earth.

At first Maffee had worked hard with the team of scientists, coming up with all sorts of ideas for new weapons such as stealth laser guns, micro rocket ships and anti-matter missiles. But as he worked on these new and great devices he began to realise his true passion. He started by keeping his own desk spotlessly clean. All his papers were neatly filed, memory pods always cleaned and his desk polished every night. However, very soon he began to clear up after other people too. If he saw an empty mug on a desk he would take it to the kitchen and give it a wash, he would stay behind after everyone else went home, so that he could vacuum the floors, empty the bins and dust the filing cabinets. After a few months he was doing less and less weapon designing and more and more tidying and cleaning for the team. Finally, when he was doing no real work at all, the head of the SWORD team called Maffee into her office.

Mo Draper was tall, beautiful, and extremely intelligent, and she was Maffee's boss. She was sat at her desk talking to her computer, discussing complex mathematical formulae. Papers, memory pods and files surrounded her, on her desk and on the floor.

Maffee knocked at her office door and it slid open.

"Come in Maffee," said Mo. "I'm just finishing this off."

Maffee walked carefully, trying not to tread on any of Mo's work. Once in the centre of the room, in front of her desk, he bent down to pick up some of the papers.

"Leave it!" Mo ordered without looking away from her computer. "Just sit down and don't tidy anything."

Maffee sat down on the chair across from Mo's desk, looking at all the mess. He crossed his arms as he desperately tried not to start sorting out his boss's papers. Why are humans so untidy, he thought. He looked out of the large window that crossed the entire length of the room. He made a mental note to give it a good clean later. The pictures of flowers and tall grass on the wall seemed out of place among the glass and metal of the modern office. In all the other offices in the building the bright blue light of the digital office clock was the only piece of furniture that provided a change of colour from shining silver and chrome.

"Computer, run that for me and hold the results until I get back to you," Mo said, and then she swivelled her chair around to face Maffee. "Now then Maffee," she smiled as she spoke. "How many projects do we have on the go at the moment?"

Maffee blinked as his internal memory checked and then said, "Seven Miss Draper."

"Right. And how many are you working on Maffee?"

"Well, all of them."

"All of them," Mo repeated. "So, what was your last contribution to the SWORD team's work then Maffee?"

"Well, I did the… I worked on the… let me see…"

6

"Maffee, you have the galaxy's most advanced brain, but you can't remember what you're working on because you haven't done any work for the past two months. Instead you've cleaned, dusted and filed for the rest of the team," her smile had faded. She seemed to be getting a little angry and Maffee was getting a little nervous. "Over the last year you've had less and less input into the team's work and you've increasingly been doing housework. Why Maffee?"

Maffee thought about this, and all he could say was, "I like it. I like to keep things clean and tidy. All this mess around, how can anyone work?" He looked around at the disorder of Mo's office.

"Are you telling me that I'm not doing my job properly?" she asked.

Maffee shifted uncomfortably in his chair.

"Oh no Miss Draper, I didn't mean you, or anyone in the team. I just meant I don't like to see untidiness and I enjoy keeping things orderly and clean."

"So what should I do? The most advanced weapons designer on my team isn't doing any designing. You're not doing what you were made to do Maffee. That means you're malfunctioning, which in turn means you're no longer able to do your job and therefore no use to my team. And when that happens, I'm supposed to tell headquarters, who will send you to the Expired Goods department for evaluation. Once you're there they'll probably take you apart, use your brain for a traffic control computer and send your body off to be recycled."

Maffee was now shaking.

"However, the team likes having you around. You do a good job of keeping things neat and tidy and in their place. That helps the team to work more efficiently," she paused. "So I'm not going to tell HQ about your change of behaviour. I'm going to keep you on, and you can continue to look after the team. You will now be responsible for all cleaning duties and helping them to organise all their files."

She was smiling now and Maffee was beaming so broadly he thought he might pop a rivet. "There are however, two special

7

conditions to this deal."

"Oh yes Miss Draper, anything, anything," said Maffee.

"Firstly, I want you to help me keep all of my work in order too. I never seem to have time to file things properly, or label my pods, or look in my in-tray regularly, in fact, I can't even see my in-tray anymore."

Maffee looked at the piles of papers on her desk and tried to guess where the in-tray might be.

"So, I want you to be responsible for my administrative duties."

Mo sat forward towards Maffee and then lowered her voice as she continued to talk. "The second thing I need from you Maffee, is top secret. You mustn't mention this to anyone."

Maffee sat up straighter to listen more carefully.

"I need you to help me with a design I'm working on. It's more advanced than anything we've worked on before. If it's successful it will be the greatest advance in space travel since light speed. But, if it fell into the wrong hands, the consequences could be disastrous for the whole Universe. So no-one else knows about this except the head of the Department of Extreme Secret Operations."

"But I'm no good at designing anymore. I just don't seem to be able to concentrate on that sort of thing."

"Don't worry. I only need you to store the data on. This project is too confidential to store in the central computer back-up drives. Your memory is large enough to cope with the information and more importantly Maffee, I can trust you. Shhh!" she suddenly said, holding a finger to her lips. She stood up and moved across the room. She paused and then pressed the yellow panel next to the door. As it slid open, a small hovering robot, the size of a shoebox beeped twice and then said

"Auto mainframe back-up procedure."

"You're early," said Mo. But the shoebox robot simply beeped twice more and repeated its statement,

"Auto mainframe back-up procedure," and then floated past Mo, into the room and settled behind her computer. A thin rod came out from the robot and inserted into a port in the back of the computer. All of the information from the computer's "common directories" was quickly copied by the robot who would take the information and transfer it to the central computer storage facility on the 47th floor of the building.

The robot retracted its needle and left the room. Mo pressed the yellow panel and the door slid closed.

"Hmph!" she said. But Maffee didn't know what she had against the robot, after all, it was just doing its job.

* * * * *

That was how Maffee had become responsible for all domestic duties around the department, and for the next three months he went to Mo's office each night to store the secret files that she had been working on that day.

* * * * *

It was eight o'clock in the evening. Maffee picked up the bags of rubbish he had collected and carried them back to the waste disposal room. He dropped them into the disposal shoot and let the lid close. As it clanked shut he stopped. He heard footsteps coming around the corner of the corridor. From the sound of them there were at least six sets of feet. It was strange, thought Maffee, at that time of night there was usually only Mo left in the office. He moved slowly towards the door, but something about the sound of the footsteps stopped him from opening it. They were sinister, marching footsteps that didn't belong in this building. The footsteps grew louder as they got nearer to the waste disposal room. Maffee froze, not wanting to make a sound, fearing the footsteps would stop outside of his room. They reached the room where Maffee was stood, but they didn't slow down, they continued past, towards the main offices where Mo was working.

There was a loud bang as they kicked open the door to her

office. Maffee jumped at the noise.

Mo jumped too, but quickly recovered. In front of her were six large figures dressed all in black, with dark, hooded cloaks that covered their faces in shadow, making them unrecognisable. "What's going on? Who are you?" she demanded.

The figures remained silent. Then, two of them moved towards her, around each side of her desk. One of them took a canister from inside his cloak. He aimed it towards Mo's face and out came a short burst of spray. But she was already moving swiftly out of her seat, knocking it backwards. She ducked under the arm of the other figure and moved toward the door, her reflexes taking over from her fear. But there was nowhere for her to go. The four other figures blocked her exit. She was grabbed from behind. The first figure stood in front of her again and this time the spray didn't miss. In the blink of an eye Mo slumped, unconscious.

Maffee heard the commotion. He knew it was coming from his boss's office and knew he should run to help her. Instead he stood rooted to the spot by his trembling metal legs. He began to make strange whimpering sounds, a mixture of fear and regret, regret that he was too scared to help poor, lovely Mo. And he whimpered some more.

Then he stopped as he heard the footsteps coming back along the corridor. He continued to listen as they grew louder, passed by the door of his room and then faded as they moved away.

It was at least an hour before he stopped shaking and two hours before he dared to open the door and look outside. The building was completely silent. Slowly he started to walk towards Mo's office, forcing himself to keep moving forward, afraid of what he might find. The door to Mo's office was wide open, the light-panels in the ceiling were on but there was no sound. He peered through the doorway. There was no one there. Then he noticed the desk was empty and her computer was also gone.

"Oh dear," he said to himself. "Oh dear, oh dear. They've taken her, and you let them do it Maffee. Why didn't you do something to stop them?" he paused to think, then answered his own question, arguing with himself. "But what could I do?" He stared around the empty room. "You're a coward Maffee, a stupid coward and now everyone is going to know it. You're no good at your job and the one person who gave you a chance to do what you wanted to do instead of sending you to the scrap yard where you belong, has been taken away because you did nothing. Well there will be no second chances for you Maffee."

He stood in Mo Draper's office thinking of his fate and thinking about what might have happened to Mo. Where had they taken her? What did they want with her? Why Mo? She was too kind and too nice to have enemies. Why would anyone want to hurt her? The reason came to him in a flash. The secret weapon! He remembered Mo's own words, "If it fell into the wrong hands, the consequences could be a disaster for the whole Universe."

"So the whole Universe is at stake and it's your fault," he continued to talk to himself. "Oh, this just gets worse. They'll melt my body and recycle it to make tins for pet food."

He decided there and then that there was only one way out of this. He would have to find Mo himself and rescue her from whoever had taken her so that everything was back to the way it was.

Chapter Two

Maffee stepped onto the moving walkway that led towards Peggy Robottom's General Store. Peggy was Maffee's only friend. He owned the shop where Maffee bought all his cleaning products and that is how they had met. When Maffee first went into Peggy's shop there was only a small selection of cleaning products: a few liquids, two or three sprays, cleaning cloths and some sponges. Maffee had begun talking to Peggy by asking him if he could get more specific products such as ink remover, carpet shampoo, non-abrasive dish cloths, anti static dust wipes and dozens of other specialised cleaning products.

They soon became friends and when Maffee went to collect his weekly supplies, he would spend a while chatting to Peggy about this and that. They'd talk about the weather, or sometimes about sport, which Maffee knew very little about, but he liked Peggy's company so he would nod as if he was interested while Peggy spoke enthusiastically about the latest sporting events. Other times they would discuss the day's news, or Peggy would tell Maffee about other cities and planets he had visited. And that was why Maffee was going to see Peggy now. With such knowledge of different places, Maffee was sure that Peggy would know where he should begin his search for Mo.

Maffee stepped off the moving walkway that transported people around the city and walked down the side street until he came to Peggy's shop. It was closed of course. It was still only five o'clock in the morning. The sun was just beginning to light up the sky. The dull outline of the large, old trees that lined the street looked out of place next too the modern glass buildings that extended high into the sky. The floating street lights were beginning to dim their power, like fading flying saucers, high above the road. Maffee decided to wait for Peggy to arrive.

At eight o'clock Peggy's autocar pulled up outside of the shop. Peggy was a normal looking human being, not very tall or short, fairly slim, with dark black hair, slicked down across his forehead.

"Hello Maffee. You must be desperate for that lemon scented furniture cream that you ordered. Come in," Peggy pressed a button on his key fob and the front door opened as the shutters of the shop drew aside.

Maffee closed the door behind him as they walked inside the shop and hesitated at Peggy's words. "Oh yes, the furniture cream, has it arrived yet?" Maffee said, remembering he had ordered it a few days ago.

"Sure, it arrived yesterday. I was going to call you today and let you know it was here. So how come you're out so early?"

"I just have a lot to do today," Maffee wasn't used to telling lies. He'd never needed to in the past, but right now he didn't feel like telling anyone what a coward he had been and the trouble he was in.

"Right. Dirt and germs wait for no man. Here's your cream," Peggy placed a small jar onto the counter and continued to chat to his friend. "So what are you up to today?"

"Well, I've been given a special assignment from Miss Draper," Maffee said, putting his plan into action.

But Peggy interrupted, "That's your boss lady. The one you've got the hots for right?"

"I have the utmost respect for her and admire her brilliant intelligence."

"OK, but we humans call that having the hots for someone," Peggy laughed at his own humour.

"Anyway," said Maffee trying to get back to the conversation. "She's asked me to conduct some research into the weapons used in today's society. So I'm going to interview people who use weapons on a daily basis."

Peggy looked puzzled. "Well that's either police troopers or hardened criminals!"

"That's it. That's exactly right. Hardened criminals are who I'm after. You know this city, where would I find that sort of people?"

"What? Are you pulling my leg Maffee? Is this one of your

13

weird robot jokes that are never funny?"

"Oh no Peggy. This is serious research. I need to know where I can find hardened criminals," Maffee hadn't thought about who he was looking for, but Peggy's description seemed perfect. Who else would be so nasty as to kidnap Mo Draper, it had to be hardened criminals.

"Well you're the boffins. I guess you know what you're doing. The best place to go would be the Treman Quarter. You'll find every type of low-life outlaw down there. There are petty criminals, thieves, murderers, hijackers, spies and the most wanted men on the planet. Just go into any of the bars down there and you'll have all the interviews you want. But I imagine that the type of person you'll interview would be just as happy to shoot you down with a single laser bolt as answer your questions."

Maffee looked worried. He hadn't really thought through his plan. He had intended to find out from Peggy where to meet a few criminals and then just do some investigating for clues. He certainly hadn't planned on being shot with laser bolts.

Peggy continued to talk, "Even the police troopers won't go there unless there's a whole group of them. If that's where you're heading, make sure you take extra care. I don't want to be called down by the troopers to identify a pile of Maffee-metal with a jar of furniture cream on the top."

"Oh don't you worry about me. I can take care of myself in the Treman Quarter or any other quarter for that matter. There's an old saying that the pen is mightier than the sword."

"Well just remember that no-one uses pens anymore and swords these days come with a 1200 mega-hertz laser-charge attached."

Chapter Three

Maffee flew out of the door and crashed down onto the dusty road with a loud "crack." Sparks flew as his metal body bounced and then landed again with a final crunch.

"Man that had to hurt. I've seen aliens beat up, busted up and stitched up on 43 different planets and I *know* that had to hurt."

Maffee looked up and saw a large Pervian Bear looking down at him. He was immediately dazzled by the bear's knee length silver shorts, silver unbuttoned waistcoat and silver cowboy hat. The bulging pockets on both the trousers and the waistcoat made the creature look even bigger.

"Actually it didn't hurt. I'm a mechanoid android feature five eight extended and I don't possess pain sensors, therefore I don't feel pain," Maffee paused. "However, I do feel a little dizzy and confused. That big bully in there must have scrambled my circuits temporarily."

"I'm not surprised. You're skinnier than a Zarvian stick insect on emergency rations. Man, I could pick you up and use you to clean the exhaust of my lightship," the big bear bent down and effortlessly picked up Maffee by the back of his neck with one orange paw and stood him on his feet.

"I only wanted to ask him a few questions, the big Cretchnian lump," Maffee said, looking back at the door he had just been thrown out of.

"This must be your first time in the Quarter. So let me give you a tip, most of the characters around here don't like being asked questions, especially by strangers. No wonder you got thrown out. You should have spoken to the barman first, he might have warned you."

"It was the barman who ejected me from that hideous establishment!" said Maffee as he stretched and moved his arms and legs, making sure everything was still in working order.

"Well, I'm not surprised at that either if you went in there talking in that fancy style. There must be over a hundred different species of alien in this Quarter and I don't know one of them that would say they were "ejected from this establishment." If you were thrown out, just say you were thrown out and tell it like it is. That way, you can avoid getting "ejected" from anywhere else.

"Hmph!" Maffee was still not happy by the way that he had been treated.

"So what's a fancy talking dude like you doing in the Quarter? You sure don't look like you have any business down here."

"If you must know, I'm looking for someone."

"Who?"

"No-one you'd know."

"How do you know who I know? You might be surprised. I know a lot of people, that's my job, to know things and see things. I have a trained eye."

"Oh really?" Maffee said. "So what is your job?"

"I'm a crime fighter, a wrong righter. I shake down crime and take out the grime. Where evil is hiding, I come in riding. Where the bad dudes are staying, I come in blazin'. If you're no good brother, you better stay under cover, because I'm a Kung Fu fighter with more moves than Michael Jackson. I'm quicker than fast food and I'm known throughout the Universe as Chuttle, the number one Space Detective."

"You've been practising that, haven't you?"

"Well yes, but I like my clients to know what they're getting for their money."

Maffee couldn't believe his luck. This big creature had some corny lines, but if this was a Space Detective then that was just what he needed. He decided to find out more. "So how many clients have you had?"

Chuttle paused before he answered, "I can't tell you that, it's confidential client information."

16

"Ok, what sort of crimes have you tackled?"

"I can't tell you that either," he said, his eyes shifting from Maffee.

"Well how many criminals have you caught?"

Chuttle shifted uneasily on his big feet. "It's hard to say."

"Oh good grief! This is ridiculous. If you're a Space Detective then I'm a chocolate frog. I'm in a very serious situation. I need to find someone who has been taken by some men who I didn't like the look of at all. Now I don't know what they might be doing to her, but I do know that the whole Universe could be at stake and I don't have time to stand here talking to you, when you are clearly not a Crimeboy Fighting Space thing at all."

Chuttle's ears had pricked up and his eyes opened wide. "The whole Universe is at stake?" he asked.

"That's right, the whole Universe and I'm the only one who knows about it."

"Oh boy, you're gonna need some help. If the Universe is at stake it will take more than one skinny roboflop to save the day."

"Hah! I trust you are joking. How could you help?"

"Ok." Chuttle said quietly. "I haven't actually caught any criminals yet. The only jobs I've had are delivering parcels across the galaxy and for the last three months I've been looking after the four-year old son of a couple of rich Sharags from the planet Sharg. But I am the fastest gun in the Western Galaxy and I have travelled around a lot in my ship, so I know a lot of things that go on in different parts of the galaxy. And I know I was born to be a Space Detective and one day save the Universe. This could be my chance, let me help you."

Maffee thought about this. He was in a place where he couldn't even ask a question without being thrown out of a building. He didn't know who he was looking for or what to do next. He needed help. "Ok. I'm looking for some men. They're dressed in black and they've kidnapped one of the government's top scientists. Do you know who they might be?"

Chuttle thought carefully and then said, "No."

"I knew this wouldn't work."

"Slow down partner, slow down. Start at the beginning. Tell me what happened."

Maffee sighed and began to tell Chuttle about the previous night. When he had finished, Chuttle said "Ahh man, why didn't you do something to stop them? If it was me I'd have run in there and triple kicked the first three then used some of my special moves to wipe out the other dudes. They wouldn't have had time to even think about it!" Chuttle stopped talking to demonstrate some of his "special" moves. A few punches in the air and a full spinning kick. When he finished he continued talking. "I can see why you had to run away, oh the shame of it, hiding away in a cupboard. If the authorities found out they'd have you turned into scrap metal quicker than you could wrap a turkey in cling film."

"You're not really making me feel any better," Maffee said. "How about trying to actually help?"

"Are you sure you didn't see anything else? You didn't get to see a face, even for a second?"

"No."

"Well were there no badges or emblems on their clothing?"

"No."

"And they were all dressed the same? All in black?"

"That's right," Maffee paused, then said, "Except, I did catch a glimpse of the last two as they went around the corner of the corridor. I think they had gold boots on."

"Gold boots, gold boots..." Chuttle said slowly. "I've got it! About nine months ago I was delivering a package from Sharg to a company on Brillon. Finding the office turned out to be easy because it was the tallest building on the planet. I could almost see it as I was

18

passing the planet's third moon. So I was leaving this package at reception and just looking around, when I see this guy coming out of the lift surrounded by about four guys in suits and another six dudes dressed in cloaks, all black except for their gold boots. I asked the receptionist who it was 'cos I was thinking he looked like one important dude and maybe if I went over and introduced myself I might be able to do some work for him. But then, as I was watching him, he turned and looked straight at me, just for a second, and let me tell you, he was one mean looking dude, his look could have turned fresh cheese into stale salami."

"So who was it?"

"The girl on reception told me it was Gelt Blista."

"Gelt Blista? The owner of Blista Mines and Blista Enterprises? One of the most successful businessmen of the century. What would he have to do with all this?"

"I don't know. I'm just telling you what I saw," Chuttle turned and started to walk away from Maffee.

"Where are you going?" Maffee cried, suddenly afraid that he was going to be left by the only help he had.

"Come on," said Chuttle. "We can talk on the way."

"On the way where?" asked Maffee as he started to walk to catch up.

"I don't know. But my dad always said there's no point in standing still. If you're walking, then at least you're getting somewhere."

Maffee ran to catch up with Chuttle, not wanting to get into anymore trouble on his own. "By the way…who is Michael Jackson?" he asked.

Chapter Four

The street they walked down was brown with dust. It wasn't like the moving fastways that Maffee was used to. The buildings were very different too. Instead of tall glass and metal skyscrapers, with well-dressed business people dashing in and out, there were small, run-down brick buildings with metal bars over windows which had mostly been painted black to stop unwanted eyes from seeing who was inside. Most visitors to the Tremen Quarter preferred privacy. Their business was their own and generally illegal. The only thing that was really different about each shop was the painted sign above them and there was a certain similarity to these too. There were a lot of pubs, quite a few food-stops and most of the other shop signs said "Hardware."

"Do a lot of tradesmen come here?" asked Maffee.

"Tradesmen? I doubt it." replied Chuttle without stopping.

"Well, why are there so many hardware shops?"

"Oh man. You really have got a lot to learn. Come on," Chuttle crossed the road and headed towards the nearest shop with a Hardware sign above it. Maffee followed close behind.

"What are we doing?"

"Showing you the hardware shop."

"I haven't got time to look at tools. I'm not interested in tools." Maffee said, already getting frustrated with Chuttle.

"If you're looking for Blista's men, you'll need to get interested, because from what I've heard, these tools are their favourite subject."

"What?" Maffee was confused, but before he could ask anything else, Chuttle was already walking into the hardware shop. So Maffee followed.

Inside the run-down shop, there were a few saws and hammers, a small selection of power tools hanging on a wall and a couple of grey shelves with screws, nails and other small items. Cracked paint was peeling from the walls and the uncovered floorboards didn't look like they had been cleaned since the twenty-first century. Maffee didn't think much of this shop. Peggy's shop was always spotlessly clean and crowded with goods for sale, this place had hardly anything in stock. He looked across to the other side of the shop and saw a small, green Brevetar shopkeeper stood behind an almost empty counter.

Chuttle walked up to the counter and Maffee followed, still confused about what they were doing in the shop. The shopkeeper looked at them both very carefully, then said without smiling, "How can I help you?"

"Hi. My friend here is interested in your hardware," answered Chuttle nodding in Maffee's direction.

"Do you have anything in particular in mind?" the shopkeeper was looking at Maffee, but it was Chuttle who answered.

"No, he hasn't decided what he wants, just show us what you've got."

The shopkeeper looked at Chuttle, then looked at Maffee and studied him for a couple of seconds, as if trying to make his mind up about something. Then he said "ok" and reached down behind his counter and flicked a switch. At first nothing happened, then there was a whirring sound as the counter top span over to reveal a second counter top full of small hand weapons. Before Maffee had a chance to look at them closely, he heard a series of loud clanks as the walls of the shop also revolved to reveal racks of weapons in a range of sizes and types. From his work as a weapons designer, Maffee had been programmed with the knowledge of all known weapons in the galaxy, and he saw a lot of them in front of him now: stealth rifles, hand lasers, rapid fire pulse guns, programmable rocket launchers, even a laserball shoulder canon that Maffee himself had designed. He turned back to the counter to look at its contents. There were small handguns, stealth laser pistols and a range of laser swords, steel knives and solid beam rapiers.

Maffee suddenly became very nervous. Although he worked as a weapons designer, the sight of a weapon outside of the laboratory always made him nervous. In the laboratory, weapons were only used in very controlled conditions, but in the outside world any fool could pull a trigger. As he studied the weapons on display, his internal video-mail beeped, making him jump. It beeped again and the shopkeeper and Chuttle looked at Maffee expecting him to answer it. Maffee blinked and sent an internal signal to his v-phone unit. The video screen on the back of his hand lit up with Peggy's face.

"Hello?" said Maffee.

"Hey Maffee. Just checking up on you, making sure you're still alive. So what do you think of the Quarter? Plenty of dirt on the streets, I bet you'd love to clean up the place."

"Well it's not quite what I expected."

"Have you found those armed criminals you're after?"

The shopkeeper was watching Maffee suspiciously.

"No not exactly. I think I'd better go now Peggy, bye."

"Say, what's going on here?" asked the shopkeeper. "Are you undercover troopers?"

From the look on his face and the tone of his voice - and of course, the shop full of illegal weapons - Maffee guessed that he didn't like police troopers.

"Don't be crazy dude!" Chuttle answered. "Do we look like troopers? Of course not," he answered his own question. "No way man, we've got a hundred and ten better things to do with our time than go around being a trooper with a sad uniform and a funny walk, picking on innocent shopkeepers who are trying to earn an honest day's pay."

"Well what was that all about?" the shopkeeper asked, pointing at Maffee's v-phone. "You troopers don't belong in the Quarter."

"Well really!" said Maffee. "Firstly, as you've already been told, we are not troopers. And secondly, as an employee of the intergalactic government, I am fully entitled to go wherever I wish. And although I would rather be in any other place than this outdated

22

ghetto, if I choose to come here, I shall."

The shopkeeper stared at Maffee and as he did, his skin started turning darker and darker. The two nodules on the top of his head started to grow upwards into two short horns, his eyes seemed to bulge out of his head and his lips drew back to reveal sharp, grey teeth. "Why you little, tin-pot, toothpick, if you're not troopers then there's no reason why I can't blast you out of my store and into galaxy dust."

Maffee felt his knees start to tremble and heard his whole body start to rattle. But it was Chuttle who spoke. "There is one reason. You see, the type of government work my friend here is involved in isn't widely known about, that's the way intergalactic secret agents work."

The shopkeeper turned to look at Maffee who stared at Chuttle wondering what this story was all about. But Chuttle continued to talk. "And the thing about being a secret agent is that they really don't like other people knowing that that is what they are. It defeats the purpose of being a secret agent. You see? So now we have a problem, because you know that he is a secret agent."

Maffee blinked, trying to take in what it was that Chuttle was talking about. And in that blink of a mechanical eye, Chuttle reached into the inside of his waistcoat, whisked out a small silver weapon and pointed it to the shop assistant's head. Maffee recognised the weapon straightaway, it was a SW Pulse Infuser, the most powerful handgun of its size. Only a few had been made as prototypes by the manufacturer before the accountants at the firm decided that they were too expensive to build. The weapon worked by drawing in the light available around it and condensing it into a single shot of energy, before releasing it. On impact with its target the shot of energy would expand, destroying whatever surrounded it - in this case, the shop assistant's head, *if* Chuttle pulled the trigger. The shop assistant obviously recognised the weapon too, his head immediately transformed back to its less intimidating features "Forgive me, I didn't mean to pry into your business. Believe me I'm extremely discreet, I never give away the identity of anyone who comes into my store, your secret is safe with me. Please, accept this as a token of my sincere apology," he began to reach into the counter full of small weapons.

"Hold it," said Chuttle. "Be very careful."

The shopkeeper's hand slowed down as he continued to reach into the cabinet and draw out a small grey, metal object. "This is the latest solid beam mini-rapier. If I ever tell anyone you were here, you can come back and chop off my horns with it."

Chuttle looked at the shopkeeper then looked at the weapon before taking it with his free hand. "OK. But if you tell anyone that the deadly Stealth Assassin was here...oh shoot! Now I've given away his secret code name as well." Chuttle winked at Maffee. "What do you want me to do now sir?" Chuttle looked at Maffee. "Do you trust him, or should I waste him right now?"

The shopkeeper was now terrified and looked ready to cry. Maffee was still amazed by the story that Chuttle had told but he guessed that the only way out of this situation was to join in with Chuttle's deception. "I think we can trust him."

Chuttle lowered his gun. "I guess you get to keep your head on your shoulders for another day. But be aware chump, we have eyes and ears everywhere," then he said to Maffee "Shall we go now?"

"I think we should."

Maffee and Chuttle turned and started to walk to the door. Maffee couldn't wait to get outside, but just as he reached the door, Chuttle turned back to the shopkeeper and asked, "Say, do you get any of Gelt Blista's men in here?"

"No." replied the shopkeeper. "They never come in here, but they do use the Riverside Inn, at the end of the street, whenever they're in the Quarter."

Chuttle nodded, and then turned back to the door. Maffee opened it and they both walked back onto the street. Maffee walked quickly away from the hardware store until he felt they were far enough away "What was all that about secret agents, you almost got us killed back there."

"No. *You* almost got us killed with your v-mail buddy. I stopped us from getting killed."

"No. You almost got us killed by taking me into that place.

24

Why couldn't you just have told me what was in there instead of introducing me personally to our friendly neighbourhood arms dealer?"

"I thought it would do you good to see for yourself. It's the best way to learn."

"You mean it's the best way to end up dead! Don't ever take me anywhere like that again."

"Oh come on. You've got to admit it was fun wasn't it? Did you see the way that guy was shaking when I told him you were the Stealth Assassin? He was so scared he would have licked your boots clean and paid you to let him. You have to learn to be cool, enjoy the moment."

"Enjoy the moment? Oh really..." Maffee was too angry to think of anything else to say, so he quickened his pace.

"Good thinking," said Chuttle. "Let's get to that bar."

"What! Wait just a minute. I don't think I could face another encounter like that."

"Relax Maffee my friend. We'll just go in there for a drink and have a look around. See if we can spot any of Blista's men and pick up any clues. There won't be any trouble, just try to be like me, cool as a wind chill."

Chapter Five

Black, leather boots, highly polished, marched down the corridor of the SWORD department, turned into the open doorway of Mo Draper's office and stopped.

"So what have we got here men?" The voice and the boots belonged to Detective Freemore Lychee of the Police Criminal Investigations Section. From his bald head, extra-long, pointed nose and tiny ears, it was obvious he was from the small planet Aurea.

The other two people in the room were both troopers. The older one answered. "Mo Draper. Head of Secret Weapons Operations Development for the past three years. Single, lives alone, works long hours. She was last seen working in this office last night. This morning staff came in and saw her door on the floor and the office in a mess. The only thing missing from the room is her computer."

"Has everyone else turned up for work?" asked Detective Lychee.

"Everyone else is in except for her assistant," replied the younger trooper.

"Who's he, or she?"

"Neither. The assistant is an 'it'. A mechanical android called Maffee. Apparently manufactured as a super-intelligent weapons designer for the government. Only, this one malfunctioned and has been kept on as a cleaner."

The older trooper interrupted. "Typical. We have the only government in the galaxy that spends three million credits to produce a cleaning robot."

"Oh, not just a cleaner," the first trooper said smiling, "this one also cooks!"

"Alright you two, that's enough," Detective Lychee wasn't smiling. "Remember, it's the same government that also pays your wages. Now where is this cleaner, Maffee?"

"He lives here in the building, but no-one has seen him today.

The only time he leaves is to pick up cleaning supplies from a shop a few streets away, so he could be there. Apparently he often spends quite a while there, talking to the shop owner."

"Send someone down to this shop and see if the cleaner is there. And let me know straight away. Now, do we have a motive - why would anyone take her away?"

"One of the workers said he thinks she might have been working on a secret project. He was in her office one day and saw some drawings on her desk and they didn't look like anything that anyone else in the team was working on."

"So she could be working on it for someone else, terrorists or another government, whoever the highest bidder is. Or maybe someone found out about her secret project and wants it for themselves." Detective Lychee was thinking aloud. Going through all the options until he found the answer he was looking for. "Make enquiries at InterEarth Government Headquarters, find out who is responsible for the SWORD team and ask if Draper was working on anything special for them that no-one else here knows about."

The younger trooper immediately headed out of the office, taking his v-mail unit out of his pocket as he left the room. Detective Lychee sighed and sat down on Mo Draper's chair while the other trooper started to look through some of the papers scattered around the floor. After about twenty minutes the first trooper came back into the office holding out the v-mail unit towards Detective Lychee. "It took me ten minutes to find the right person to talk to and another ten to get them to understand that we're dealing with a possible kidnapping. Then this guy demanded that he speak to you sir."

"Who is it?" Detective Lychee snapped. He didn't like government departments. They were slow at making decisions and usually made the wrong ones. Before the trooper could answer, Lychee had grabbed the v-mail unit and held it up in front of his face. "This is Detective Lychee, who are you?"

"Roland Cobber, Head of Defence Strategy. Are you in charge of finding Miss Draper?" the face that Detective Lychee saw on the screen in front of him was a big dark face with rosy cheeks and large glasses.

Both men were already nearly shouting at each other. Cobber obviously didn't like police troopers anymore than Detective Lychee liked government officials.

"Yes, I'm in charge and I need to know what Miss Draper was working on and any reason that someone would break into her office and take her away."

"Are you sure she's been kidnapped?"

"Unless she usually kicks her own door down before going home, then yes, we're pretty sure."

"Blast! Someone must have found out about it."

"About what?"

"A project she was working on for us. Top secret. I can't tell you what it is, but you must find her as quickly as possible. I've got to go, this is terrible, terrible."

Cobber hung up, leaving Detective Lychee looking at a black screen. "As helpful as ever. You get more information talking to a slice of ham than talking to those government types. Any word about the cleaner?"

"He wasn't at the shop, but the shopkeeper said Maffee was there this morning waiting for him to arrive."

"Hmm." Detective Lychee was thinking hard. "So we've got a kidnapped woman who was working on a top secret weapons project, that no-one knew about except for Cobber's department and maybe a few people in this department. The only one who isn't here today, apart from the victim, is a robot who had already been fired from his job and demoted to a cleaner. If that cleaner finds out his boss is working on something pretty racy, maybe he thinks it's payback time, revenge for being humiliated and at the same time earn himself a nice little retirement package by selling a secret weapon to the highest bidder on the black market."

Detective Lychee seemed happy with his logic. "I think I'd

better go and have a talk with the shopkeeper."

* * * * * *

When Detective Lychee walked into the shop, Peggy was near the back stacking shelves. He looked up as the detective walked inside. "Hi, can I help you?"

He put the last of the cans he was stacking onto the shelf and walked back towards his counter.

"Are you the owner?" asked Detective Lychee, not wasting time with friendly greetings.

"Yes, I'm Peggy Robottom. Is this about Maffee?" Peggy guessed from the tone of Lychee's voice that he wasn't there to buy cleaning products. The visit from the two troopers earlier in the day looking for Maffee had made him start worrying about his friend, so he guessed that the man in his shop was there for the same reason.

"I'm Detective Lychee. I heard that Maffee was in here early this morning?"

"That's right. I knew he'd get into trouble going down to the Treman Quarter on his own looking for armed criminals. Oh dear. Is he alright? What's happened?"

Without realising it, Peggy had given Detective Lychee just the sort of information he was after. He continued his questions to see what else Peggy knew. "Did he tell you why he was going to the Treman Quarter?"

"He said he was doing it for his boss at work, Mo Draper. He was trying to find some pretty dangerous people by the sound of it. He wanted do some research about weapons. I warned him it was dangerous."

This was also important news for Detective Lychee, but he didn't let his interest show. "Was Miss Draper with him?"

"No. He was on his own, as usual. I knew he shouldn't have gone there alone. That's why I called him on his v-mail. Now that I think about it, he seemed a bit odd when we spoke."

29

"In what way?"

"Kind of nervous and distracted by something else. He seemed like he wanted to get off the v-mail as quickly as possible."

"You better give me his v-mail address, we need to track him down."

"So you don't know where he is? Then how do you know he's in trouble, has he contacted you?" Peggy asked.

"We don't know if he's in trouble, yet. We just need to find him to ask him some questions. If he calls you, then contact me immediately on this number." Detective Lychee produced a card from his inside pocket and gave it to Peggy. "You know the sort of work he was involved in, so you know how important this is."

Peggy thought about it for a second then said, "He's a cleaner."

"Just call me if he shows up!" Detective Lychee turned and walked out of the shop.

Once he was back inside his car, Detective Lychee dialled Maffee's number into his car's v-mail unit. He waited a few seconds...

Maffee was stood at the far end of the bar inside the Riverside Inn. Chuttle was at the other end of the bar talking to one of the barmen. Maffee guessed that Chuttle must have been here before as he seemed to know the barman quite well, they were chatting and laughing about something. He hadn't wanted to follow Chuttle into the Inn, he didn't relish the thought of going into another bar, but based on his experiences so far in the Quarter, he didn't want to stay outside on his own either. He started to look around at the few other characters that were in the bar. There was a human or two and then some other types of aliens from various planets, but there wasn't anyone in the Inn that Maffee liked the look of, they all looked rough, dirty and very mean. Just then he got another shock as his v-mail unit rung making him jump again. Automatically he quickly answered it, not wanting the noise of his ringtone to attract anyone's attention.

Detective Lychee's head came on screen. "Are you Maffee?"

Maffee paused, then nervously said, "Yes, who are you?"

"I'm Detective Lychee, and I'm investigating the disappearance of Mo Draper, do you know her?"

Maffee began to shake again. "Err, yes, she's my boss."

"Do you know where she is Maffee?"

"No. No I don't." Maffee paused then added, "isn't she at work?"

"Maffee, she isn't at work and I think you know that she isn't at work, don't you? And you know why she isn't at work don't you Maffee?"

"Well, I…"

"Come on Maffee, don't play games with me. I know what's going on and I think we need to talk. Hand yourself in and bring Miss Draper with you. Make it easy on yourself, before this gets too serious."

"What! How can I bring Miss Draper with me, I don't know where she is!"

"Look, I know what it's like, you lost your job, and she humiliated you in front of all your work mates. Fired you from top scientist and made you a cleaner. I'd be angry too, but kidnapping her is a major crime, and you could be in real trouble unless you bring her back now."

"Kidnapped her! You think I kidnapped her! That's ridiculous. How dare you!"

"Listen Maffee, why don't you tell me where you are and I'll come and meet you. We can talk about this man to man, or man to robot!"

"Robot! I am a Mechanoid Android, not a brainless robot. And I am certainly not a kidnapper."

"Ok then, but you are the last person who saw Miss Draper,

why don't you tell me where you are and you can help me with my enquiries?" Detective Lychee was smiling, trying to be nice, hoping that Maffee would tell him where he was, then he'd have a dozen troopers down there in under a minute and the case would be over. But the next thing he saw on his video screen was a large Pervian bear's head.

"Hey who's this dude Maffee?" Chuttle asked.

"He's a detective. He thinks I've kidnapped Miss Draper!"

"Smoking Joseph! Turn it off, turn off your v-mail now!" Chuttle grabbed Maffee's wrist, covering the screen of the v-mail unit. With his other paw he was trying to find a button to hang up the call. Maffee struggled to retrieve his hand from the big bear's grip.

"Get off me will you, you big oaf," he pulled his arm free.

Detective Lychee was trying to follow what was going on, but this had become difficult when Chuttle's paw had covered the v-mail screen. All he heard was Chuttle shouting at Maffee.

"They'll trace the call, he's just keeping you talking long enough to get the troopers down here to zap your skinny, tin rear-end. Now hang up!"

Maffee looked at the screen on the back of his wrist. He blinked and sent a signal ending the call.

"Are you crazy?" Chuttle continued to shout. "I hope they didn't have time to get our position or we're in trouble. And another thing, if troopers do show up you're on your own, they're not looking for me."

"At least I know I have your support," Maffee said sarcastically. "Can we just get on with why we came here? Did you find anything out from the barman?"

"Not yet, we were just catching up, he's an old friend, come on."

* * * * *

Detective Lychee looked at the blank screen then quickly dialled another number and the young trooper from Mo Draper's office appeared. "Check with headquarters for a trace on my last call. I've found Maffee. He's working with someone else, a Pervian Bear called Chuttle. Send some troopers to pick them up."

"How will they know who to pick up?"

"It shouldn't be hard to spot a blue robot and a large Pervian bear wearing a silver waistcoat. Now get that trace and bring them both in. But be careful, these are a dangerous pair."

Chapter Six

Chuttle walked back to the barman who was busy washing glasses. Maffee followed. "Say Frasier, do you get many of Gelt Blista's men coming in here?"

"Yeah, now and again *brshhh*. They're easy to spot, all in black with gold boots and they never smile *brshhh*." The barman was a Burovian. Burovians had hard yellow skin and large mouths with big loose lips which caused a strange sound at the end of each sentence."

"Have you seen any here lately?"

"Yeah, there was a group of them in last night, but they didn't stay long *brshhh*."

"What time were they here?"

"About 8.30 brrr"

Maffee was pleased that the strange sound wasn't quite as long this time. He wondered what customers thought about being served drinks by a creature that spat every time he spoke.

Chuttle turned to Maffee and asked "What time did they take your boss?"

"Shhh! You're not supposed to tell anyone," Maffee hissed.

"I'm not telling anyone," Chuttle lowered his voice too. "And besides, I told you, people in the Quarter mind their own business. You could tell Frasier here that your middle name is Mary and he wouldn't tell a soul. Now what time were they in your office?"

"It was about 9.30"

"There it is man, I knew it!"

"What? That doesn't prove anything."

"Of course it does," Chuttle turned back to Frasier, "Did you hear what they were talking about?"

"Nope, not a word *brshhh*."

Chuttle turned back to Maffee. "See, I told you that you could trust Frasier. He won't repeat anything he hears."

"That's right. It would be a big mistake *brshhh*," said Frasier, then he added "Say, is your name really Mary?"

"Oh good grief," said Maffee and he turned back to Chuttle. "I still don't believe that a businessman like Gelt Blista could have anything to do with this."

"Well we'll soon find out, and you heard what Frasier said, Blista's men were here just before you saw them in your office."

"But I just don't see it how what you're saying can be true," Maffee protested.

"When it's cold outside, you can't see that it's cold, but you know it is cold, right?"

"Of course…"

"Exactly. You don't have to see it, you just have to know."

"But I don't know," Maffee still protested.

"Well I do and you soon will, so let's get out of here and I'll prove it to you."

"Where are we going now?" Maffee asked as confused as ever.

"To find Blista's men and hopefully your boss too."

Chuttle and Maffee said goodbye to Frasier and walked outside of the Riverside Inn. Just as they did so, three Trooper Protective Vehicles (TPVs) drove past. Chuttle and Maffee watched them as they skidded to a halt about 30 metres further down the road, and started reversing.

"Quick!" said Chuttle grabbing Maffee's arm and pulling him back inside the inn. "They traced the call, we've got to move it!"

"I don't have to run anywhere. I'll explain my story and they'll see that I don't have Miss Draper and then they can go looking for the real kidnappers."

"Listen man, do you think they sent three TPVs down here because they want to talk to you? You better shake your tail feathers dude or you're heading straight for jail time," Chuttle ran back to the bar. "Hey Frasier, do you have a car out the back?"

"Sure," he took a key from his pocket and handed it to Chuttle. "Just send it back here when you're finished *brshhh*."

Chuttle ran over to the back door. He called to Maffee without even looking back. "Come on Maffee, shake it!"

"Ohhhhh," Maffee followed Chuttle out to the back of the bar.

As they got close to the silver sports car the key in Chuttle's hand gave a single "beep" and the car doors opened. They jumped inside and the doors closed. The key beeped again and the car's engine came to life. Lights on the panel in front of them lit up. Chuttle pushed a few buttons and the car shot forward and out into the back alleyway.

Two troopers got out of each TPV and ran inside the inn. They looked around but didn't see Chuttle or Maffee. There was only one other door out of the building which they ran out of in time to see the back of Frasier's car speeding away.

It wasn't long before Chuttle saw the flashing lights of the three TPVs appear on his rear-view monitor. He pressed a few more buttons and took over the controls from the auto-steer system. Maffee braced himself by grabbing hold of his seat as Chuttle swerved between other cars and lorries. "What are we going to do now?" asked Maffee.

"We need to get out of here," said Chuttle, concentrating on the road.

"Well I'd gathered that. But how?"

"You crazy fool! Move out the way. Hot Smoking Joseph! Why don't people watch where they're going." Chuttle yanked at the steering wheel in order to avoid two cars that had pulled out in front of him as he sped through a red light.

Maffee decided to keep quiet while Chuttle was driving and just hope that they didn't crash and didn't get caught by the troopers, who were still close behind.

They raced through the streets of the Quarter for another few miles. Maffee felt dizzy from all the spinning around corners and swerving to avoid on-coming traffic. He hadn't been in a car many times in his life. He didn't have any need for them. He lived in the same building where he worked and the only place he went to was Peggy's store. Most of the times he visited Peggy's, he could carry his shopping back to the office. If he had too much to carry, Peggy would deliver it for him after he had closed the shop for the day. After this trip with Chuttle he would be quite happy never to travel in a car again. He closed his eyes tightly and gripped onto his seat as the car continued to weave in and out of traffic.

After what seemed to Maffee like a very long time, Chuttle cried, "Yes! We're here, now if I can just keep those troopers off us for a little longer…"

Maffee opened his eyes and was amazed at what he saw. In front of him was row after row of all kinds of spacecraft. There were spaceships, rocket ships, cargo ships, fighters, cruisers and transporters. They were all different colours from the shiniest of silver metal to the darkest black. Some were huge, the size of Maffee's office building, others were small, thin and obviously built for speed. Maffee was amazed. He had never seen so many spacecraft in one place. Some of them he recognised from his weapons programming, but some of them he had never seen before. He guessed they were from far-off planets carrying the strangest of alien creatures and all sorts of exotic cargo.

"What is this place?" he asked.

"It's a space-port," Said Chuttle, who was still concentrating on his driving.

"What's it for?"

"It's for all incoming space traffic. You can't have ships coming in from across the galaxy and docking wherever they want all over the planet, blocking up city centres. So they all come to places like this. Then their cargo gets picked up from here, or their passengers pick up transport to wherever they want to go."

"So what are we doing here?"

"We're getting off this planet. If I can remember where I left the Dragonfly."

"You have a Dragonfly, one of the fastest ships in the galaxy?" for the first time since they had met, Maffee was impressed by what Chuttle had said.

"Oh yeah! And once we're on it there's not a thing that can touch us."

Chuttle yanked the steering wheel again and their car twisted in-between two large space ships. He didn't slow down as they sped past more ships and transport trucks. The car turned again, racing down another row of ships. Maffee looked on the monitor and didn't see the TPVs following them.

"How come they won't be able to catch us?"

"How come? I'll tell you how come. Because my baby has been modified to petrify, it's been hyped up to speed up with more light speed than a streak of greased up lightning and with all that power under the control of the galaxy's finest, fastest and furriest pilot, we'll be gone before they even know we've arrived."

"So where is it?"

"I can't remember. It's here somewhere. I think it's down here." Chuttle jerked at the steering column, turning the car left.

Maffee checked the rear view monitor again and saw the flashing lights of the TPVs in the background.

"There's the beauty!" Chuttle cried.

Maffee tried to see which was the Dragonfly. He had heard of them, but had never seen one. A sleek, shiny, red rocket ship caught his eye. It had two large booster rockets on either side of a tall pointed body. Chuttle raced towards it.

He slammed on the breaks in the middle of the roadway that they had been racing down. The doors of the car opened. "Come on!" Chuttle said as he started to get out of the car. After they were both out, he pressed a grey button on the driver's panel and the car doors closed as it moved away, back to the Riverside Bar.

Maffee began to move quickly towards the shiny, rocket ship. Chuttle began running to the other side of the road. "Where are you going?" shouted Maffee.

"To the ship. Shake it will you!" and he carried on running.

Maffee stared at the ship that Chuttle was running towards. The Dragonfly was an old, grey, small ship. It was dented in several places, as if it had been through an asteroid shower, and hadn't been washed since.

The loading door opened automatically and Chuttle climbed in. Maffee started to run across the road towards the Dragonfly and caught sight of the TPVs skidding around the corner and heading towards him. He tried to run faster, wishing that instead of spending three million credits on his brain, they had spent a little more of it on his legs. As he got to the door of the Dragonfly, the TPVs skidded to a halt where Frasier's car had stopped just seconds ago. The troopers jumped out with their weapons already drawn. A shot of laser flew past Maffee's head and hit the side of the Dragonfly. Maffee shrieked and automatically raised his arms in the air "don't shoot, don't shoot!" he cried. Another shot hit the floor by his feet. This is it, thought Maffee, they're going to kill me. But then a big orange and brown, hairy arm came out of the doorway and grabbed Maffee, dragging him into the ship.

Chuttle closed the door, with lasers still shooting into it. "Come on!" he called and ran to the front of the ship. He sat down into the pilot's seat and started to press buttons on the panels around him. Maffee, still dazed and confused, sat down in the seat next to Chuttle and quickly started to strap himself in with the seatbelts.

"Come on sugar, come on," Chuttle was pressing buttons and pushing and pulling control levers. Suddenly there was a loud crack as the engines came to life. "Oh yeah! Now we're cooking." The

Dragonfly slowly lifted off the ground and began to tilt upwards, laser shots still shooting off the front and sides of the ship.

"See ya guys!" Chuttle pushed a lever forward and the Dragonfly blasted into the sky. The force pushed Maffee deep into his seat.

Chapter Seven

A large face, with greasy skin and dark, greasy hair was inches from Mo Draper. The breath coming from it smelt of old, stale food. Mo Draper was sat on a chair. Her hands were tied behind her back and her feet were tied together. In front of her was Gelt Blista.

She couldn't see the room very clearly, it was too dark. The only light came from a dim light on the ceiling. Two guards stood by the door and that too had no window. The only other furniture in the room was a small table in the corner which was empty and the hard, cold chair that didn't offer Mo any comfort.

"You know who I am don't you Miss Draper?"

"Of course."

Everyone knew Gelt Blista. He was often on aerovision, or in the news for some new business venture or for setting up a new charity or giving money away to help others. Mo couldn't understand why she had been kidnapped, tied to a chair and was now looking at him face to face. She tried to clear her head and control her fear.

"And you know why I've brought you here?" Blista asked.

"No I don't. I don't know what's going on, but you better have a very good reason for kidnapping me and bringing me here, wherever we are."

"Come, come Miss Draper. You're an extremely intelligent woman. In fact, so intelligent that no other person could help my organisation."

"Well if you're offering me a job, I think you need some help with your recruitment technique. A simple letter mentioning a large salary and luxury apartment would have done the trick."

Blista smiled with his lips pressed tightly together, eyebrows raised and eyes wide open. It was the sort of smile that would make a baby cry.

"No, Miss Draper. I know you too well. I know your type. You believe in doing the right thing. In supporting just causes and protecting the weak and innocent. You would never agree to help me build a fleet of JXX7s would you?"

Mo was shocked. She said nothing, but couldn't believe that anyone else knew about the secret project she was working on. Even though Blista was one of the Galaxy's richest and most powerful businessmen, he shouldn't have known about the secret project. She tried to think of how Blista could know about it. The only people involved were a few people at the Defence Strategy department and Maffee. "I don't know what you're talking about," Mo said.

"Oh well I think you do. After all, who else could develop such a weapon? The files on your computer will provide plenty of proof that you know exactly what I'm talking about. Oh, and don't worry about the electronic protection, my technical people are already working on cracking your system."

Mo didn't know what to say. Blista obviously knew about the JXX7 so there was no point denying it anymore. "Well if you have the files, you can go ahead and build the JXX7s. Why am I here?"

"Do you realise, I'm one of the richest beings you will ever meet? But with all this wealth, there is one thing that I still can't buy. Do you know what it is?"

"Love?"

"No no no. Love is for failures who can't succeed in life. What I desire, but my money has so far failed to buy me, is *absolute* power. I have power, but not enough. I own companies, planets and even people, but I don't yet own the entire Galaxy. And I could you know, with the right tools at my disposal, I could rule everything. The whole Galaxy, and even more."

"OK, suppose I indulge your fantasy, how do I fit in with such a grand plan?"

"You're here because I also know that the design of the JXX7 isn't complete. However, I had to get you and your computer now, because once you had finished your work you would have sent all the information to your bosses in the InterEarth government, and that would have been a waste. The government is full of half-wits and do-gooders, neither of which could ever understand the real value of what you are creating. To have the JXX7 is to hold the Galaxy in the palm of one's hand. Imagine having a spaceship that could turn itself and everyone on board into dust sized particles and then travel anywhere at speeds that have never been thought of, avoiding detection from any radar or security systems, before re-appearing wherever you wanted to be. A ship such as that could turn slaves to kings and, of course, kings to slaves in a day. Well I am tired of being a slave to the governments of Earth and the rest of the planets in the Galaxy. Always having to abide by this law and that law. Always having to speak nicely to her, or to do a favour for him in order to get approval for my plans and businesses. Not being able to build where I want, or mine what I want because of protection orders or other people's rights. With a fleet of JXX7s at my disposal, I will be able to go anywhere I want. My men will be able to enter all of the major defence installations and render them useless, leaving the InterEarth government no option but to surrender to me. And then I will make the demands and I will set the laws and I will have the power!"

Mo Draper was watching Blista as he built himself up into a madman's rage. She wasn't a doctor but she thought that she could safely say that this man was definitely a nutcase. A pure fruitcake, 100 per cent cuckoo. King Crackerjack, bar none. She waited for him to calm down.

"And that's where you come in Miss Draper," he was talking calmly again. "I need you to finish your design for the JXX7 and while you're doing that, my scientists will be building the first prototype, with your help of course."

"With my help? That's not very likely. You are clearly mad. I wouldn't even help you to build a snowman, not to mention my JXX7 and you couldn't do anything to force me."

Blista turned away from Mo and nodded to one of his cloaked men stood behind him. The figure in black walked to Blista and handed him a slim, black box. Blista pressed a button at the side of the box and it opened to reveal a 3D screen. The screen lit up with an image. He held it in front of Mo's face. She immediately recognised the image in front of her and if she had been conscious of it, she would have felt all of her mental and physical strength drain away from her.

It was her parents' home on Earth. "Why are you showing me this?" she asked, trying to keep her voice from trembling.

"Keep watching." Blista said, not taking his eyes from the screen.

Mo looked back at the screen in front of her. The image began to shake. The shaking grew more violent and then suddenly the whole building exploded outwards into a million pieces. Mo watched in horror, her mouth wide open but no sound coming out. The screen filled with an image of black and grey smoke. When the smoke cleared there was nothing left of her parents' home, just a charred black hole in the ground.

"What have you done? What have you done!" she shouted and tried to pull herself free of the bindings that strapped her to the chair.

"Consider yourself fortunate. Not many people get to see into the future. Don't worry, your parents are safe, and their home is safe," Blista's smile slowly turned to an evil grimace, "as long as you help me to build the JXX7. If you don't, then what you have just seen on screen, becomes real."

Mo breathed deeply as she realised that the images were just computer graphics. A clever simulation designed to scare her, and it had worked. There were tears in her eyes.

"You need time to think about it," said Blista. "I'll leave you alone for a while, and when I return, I hope you'll see the sense in working for me. Most people usually do." He smiled that evil smile again then turned to one of his guards, "Untie Miss Draper, we must treat our employees well."

The guard removed the bindings that held Mo to the chair, but she remained where she was, still shocked by the images she had seen.

Blista and his men left the room. The door closed behind them and they continued to walk down a corridor towards the lift. "Make sure that Draper's workstation is set up with everything she'll need to complete her work. And make sure there's a guard outside her door at all times," although Blista hadn't directed his orders at anyone in particular, two of the guards turned down a separate corridor to carry

44

out his instructions. The rest of his men followed him into the lift.

Blista took his v-mail unit out of his top pocket and pressed a button. The face of an old man with a grey beard and glasses appeared on screen. "Ah Saffa, how are your men doing with Draper's computer?"

Saffa was one of Blista's top scientists. He was the man that Blista had put in charge of building the JXX7s.

"We're getting closer to accessing the security system sir," he spoke slowly, knowing that this was not the answer that Blista wanted.

"Closer? How much longer is this going to take? It's only one government computer. I've got a drinks machine that's more sophisticated," Blista's voice was starting to rise again. "I want those designs accessed by the end of tomorrow. Or I'll find another person for the job. What about the preparations for building the prototype, have you got all of the materials?"

"We have all of the equipment and materials that we think will be needed. We're waiting to see the designs before we can have everything ready."

"Saffa, you make sure that everything is ready by the end of tomorrow so that we can start work on the JXX7. I want this project up and running!" He snapped shut the v-mail unit.

The lift stopped and the door slid open. Blista walked out. In front of him was a huge hollow area the size of a hundred football pitches. It was connected by criss-cross passages, walkways and massive supporting beams. The area was dimly lit by thousands of spot lights attached to the rough, brown walls of stone that had been torn away by heavy machines. From this central, hollow point, Blista's men were mining, creating tunnels as they dug.

Blista watched scruffy men, women and children, with torn clothes covered in brown dust, moving in different directions, carrying, digging, lifting and loading. An automated wagon rolled out of one of the tunnels, its carriages filled with Rusdan crystals. These were pale brown crystals that would be crushed into powder, then encased in chrome tubes the size of a man's forearm, and used to provide power for planets throughout the galaxy. A single battery provided enough power to run a car for years. With five batteries a spaceship could fly from one end of the galaxy to the other. Rusdan was also used to provide power to whole cities. It was cheaper and safer than any other type of fuel and it was the key to Blista's vast fortune and power.

He had discovered a series of small planets in a corner of the galaxy that were filled with Rusdan. All he had to do was get enough labour to mine it for him. Fortunately for him, there was a bitter civil war raging on the planet Ircone. The two sides of the planet had clashed and thousands of people were desperate to find safety. Blista took transporter ships to the planet and offered them an escape. He promised them jobs that paid well, somewhere to live and safety for their families. He took hundreds of them to his mining planets and set them to work in terrible conditions. There was no way for them to leave the mines. They found themselves trapped and treated like slaves. At first many of them had protested to Blista, but he had his own way of dealing with employees who disagreed with his methods. They were beaten by guards in front of the other workers and then taken away, never to be seen again. Soon the other workers were too afraid to complain.

Because no one could leave the planet, there was no way of reporting the cruel treatment to the authorities. Blista was free to do as he pleased on his planets. To the rest of the galaxy he was a respected and admired businessman. He had cheap labour, lots of profit and he was a powerful businessman - but that wasn't enough for Gelt Blista.

Chapter Eight

The Dragonfly was cruising through space. There was no sound apart from the quiet hum of its engine. Maffee hadn't spoken since Chuttle had dragged him on-board. They both sat at the front of the spacecraft in silence. Chuttle had a big grin of delight on his face from the thrill of escaping the troopers and blasting into space. In his head, he was re-living the last few hours of excitement. First of all a car chase and then dodging the lasers of the troopers, this was the kind of action that he had always dreamed of, this was what being a space detective was all about and the adventure had just begun.

On the other hand, Maffee's silence was at first due to shock, but now he was silenced by the wonderment of space. He stared out of the window, amazed at the colour and movement of the vast sight before him. Back on Earth he had always assumed that "space" was just a big, dark void broken up by grey planets and small yellow stars. However, what he saw now filled him with wonder. The atmosphere was blue but with strange red and yellow mists floating aimlessly past his window. Each planet that he saw seemed to be a different shade: the blueness of Aquenus, the dark red of Morotto, the two-tone colour of Fra E247 which seemed to shift from green to yellow depending on which of its suns was in dominance. Shooting stars flashed across his view, burning orange with heat caused by their incredible speeds, leaving a trail of bright yellow sparks.

Occasionally he would see other spacecrafts in the distance, all different sizes and shapes travelling in different directions to who knew where. Maffee assumed that they were either cargo ships or passenger liners, or perhaps even spaceforce ships. All of them going about their business and none of them in as much trouble as he was now.

Perhaps if I were not trying to rescue Miss Draper from violent criminals whilst evading capture by the police troopers, it would be nice to spend some time in space exploring its distant reaches, Maffee thought. Perhaps when this ordeal is over and life is back to normal I'll be able to do some travelling. Maybe I could convince Peggy to accompany me. He'd certainly be a more suitable companion than this hyperactive Pervian magnet to danger.

"Beautiful isn't it?" Chuttle interrupted Maffee's thoughts. "I never get tired of travelling through space. The magnificence of it all can capture your breath and hold it so that you're in danger of never breathing again unless someone comes to lead you away."

Maffee turned to look at Chuttle who was staring out of the other window.

"Are you ok now?" Chuttle asked, but there was no response from Maffee.

"That was some chase wasn't it? It's not often that anyone gets away from three TPV's, but then again there aren't many drivers like me in the galaxy, a lethal combination of speed and control. Shizam! Now you see me, now you don't! Man, I'm glad I met you. I haven't had this much fun in a long time."

Maffee turned his head towards Chuttle and stared at him.

"What? What's up?" asked Chuttle.

"You're really enjoying this aren't you? You have no concept of the danger we've been in. Less than twenty-four hours ago I was living a comfortable and peaceful life. Then I meet you and I'm being threatened, chased, shot at and wanted for kidnapping. And why? All because you think this is one big game, well it's not a game, it's not fun and I'm not happy. And it's all because of you!"

"Hey wait a minute. Who's helping who here?"

"Well you certainly aren't helping me. Oh unless you count helping me to get thrown out of illegal arms trading shops, or helping me to get killed in a car crash, or helping me to get shot to pieces by troopers. So which one is it?"

"OK. Well I don't remember being around when you were cowering in a cupboard while your boss was being kidnapped. I wasn't around when you did nothing to stop them, or even follow them to find out where they were going. However, I do remember being with you when you were thrown out of a bar and were lying on the ground whining like a baby because you didn't know what to do next. And I think it was me who picked you up and helped make some progress on this case."

"Progress? What progress? We may be miles from where we started, but we're no nearer to finding out where Miss Draper is."

"Wrong again. We know that it was Blista's men who took her and we know why. All we have to do is find out where they took her."

"Even if it was Gelt Blista who took Miss Draper, how do we find out where she is now?"

Chuttle went quiet. He didn't have an answer to that question.

"Come on mister big shot, space detective. What do we do now?"

"Ahh, so you admit you need my help! Well partner, I'll think of something don't you worry."

Maffee sighed. He didn't have much faith in Chuttle, but once again he realised that he had no-one else to turn to for help. So instead he went back to looking out of the window. He had never been in space before and hadn't thought about what it might be like. But now he was fascinated by the darkness of the sky and the thousands of bright lights surrounding them. He tried to make out which of the lights were stars, which were planets and which were other spaceships, flying through space just like he was. Then his mind turned back to Mo Draper. He wondered whether she was on one of those planets or one of the spaceships out there. How would he ever find out? They could search forever and still not find her. And Chuttle was right, all of this had happened because he had let them take Miss Draper away. "I'm sorry." he said.

"What?" Chuttle wasn't expecting an apology.

"Sorry for blaming you. I'm just not used to all this and I don't know what I'm going to do."

"I told you. This is my chance to make a name for myself. It's my destiny and I'm not going to fail. We'll find Miss Draper and we'll get her back safely. I'll think of something."

"I hope so," then he changed the subject. "I think I need to recharge and re-stabilise my systems, do you have a socket I could use?"

"Sure, there's one back there on the left by that green box."

Maffee got up and walked over to the green box. He saw the power socket and plugged in his input cord.

Chuttle continued to pilot the ship, although not really sure where he was going.

* * * * * *

After about an hour of drifting through space, Chuttle's v-mail rang. He pressed a button and a screen on the ship's instrument panel lit up with Frasier's face.

"Hey Frasier. Did you get your car back ok?" Chuttle asked.

"Yeah sure, no problem. I take it you managed to lose the troopers *brshhh*?"

"Silly question Frasier, they were never going to catch the speed demon. So what's up?"

"You know you were asking about Blista's men *brshhh*?"

"Yep."

"Did they really take your friends boss-lady?"

"Sure did. But we'll get her back."

"Well, if I tell you something, you won't let anyone know I told you ok *brshhh*?"

"Sure. What is it?"

"When Blista's men were in here, I overheard some of their conversation. They were saying how they were pleased to be away from the mine and they weren't looking forward to going back *brshhh*."

"Do you know which mine they were talking about?"

"I'm not too good with planets but I think they mentioned, Suvmar. I hope that helps, but remember, you didn't hear it from me *brshhh*."

"No sweat buddy, thanks for this."

"Yeah, well I meet a lot of creeps working here, but I can't stand the ones who pick on defenceless women. I'll see you next time you're in town *brshhh*."

The screen went blank.

Chuttle immediately started to check on the Dragonfly's navigation system to find the planet that Frasier had mentioned. It took him a while but eventually he found it. The details provided by the navigation system were only brief. It said that Suvmar was a small, uninhabited planet hidden behind a larger planet in the corner of Sector 15 of the Charanian Galaxy. It said that it was owned by Blista Enterprises and was a mining planet, used to provide Rusdan.

Chuttle pressed a few more buttons and programmed the ship to take them on the quickest route to Suvmar.

He decided that since he had such good news, it was worth waking up Maffee. Besides, he was bored and wanted someone to talk to. He walked over to where Maffee was standing and knocked on his head. Maffee's eyes opened, "What the devil are you doing?"

"I need to tell you something."

"So you bang on my head with your fist! Are you always so polite?"

Chuttle ignored Maffee's comments and walked back to the console. "Come here, Look at this. I think I've figured out where they could have taken Miss Draper."

"What? Where? How? Show me."

Chuttle pointed to the navigation screen. "Suvmar. It's one of Blista's mining planets. It would be perfect for him to take her there. It's a tiny place, tucked away in the corner of the Charanian Galaxy and no-one else lives on the planet. He can do what he wants there without anyone else knowing."

"So you think he's taken her there?"

"Sure, it's obvious."

"Well what makes you so sure?"

"Listen, I told you when we first met, it's my job to know things. I'm a crime fighter, a wrong righter. I shake down crime and take out the grime. Where evil is hiding…"

"OK, ok. Don't start all that again. Can't you put it into normal language? How do we know they've taken Miss Draper to Suvmar?"

"Frasier told me. He v-mailed while you were recharging. Said he overheard Blista's men talking when they were in his bar."

"Well why didn't he tell us this before?"

"I told you. People from the Quarter don't talk much. It's safer that way. But he's an old friend of the Space Detective and so he got in touch."

"Right. Well I'll try and contact Detective Lychee and tell him."

"Don't be crazy. Lychee is after *you*. He's not going to send his men all the way to a distant galaxy because you say so. He thinks you're the kidnapper. If you contact him, he'll trace your call again and come looking for us. Then they'll interrogate us and maybe after a week or so of getting nowhere they'll finally believe your story and send someone to Suvmar. But by then Blista could have moved Mo somewhere else and Lychee will think you're playing games with him and we'll be back to square one. No. We've got to get her back ourselves."

Maffee didn't say anything. He knew Chuttle was right. Lychee was looking for him and wasn't going to believe a story about Gelt Blista being involved in a kidnapping plot.

"So what are we going to do? We can't just turn up on a mining planet pretending to be tourists and then ask if they have any government scientists visiting them."

"Don't worry your wiring, I've got a plan. We crash land on the planet and then while the Dragonfly is being repaired, we split up and find your boss. Then we sneak her on board and blast out of there."

Maffee looked at Chuttle in disbelief.

"Oh my word. And you really think that's a plan?"

"Sure. What's wrong with it?"

"We're going to 'crash land' on the planet? How do you crash land without getting us both killed?"

"Listen Maffee my man, I told you, you are looking at the finest pilot to ever grace the velvet skies. There's not a bird in the air that can fly better than me and not a pilot in the Universe that can match my skills. In fact I'm surprised God didn't just give me a pair of wings instead of these two arms. Trust me."

"Ohh." Maffee groaned. "Ok, let's pretend for a moment that you can simulate a crash landing and we both live through it, what happens next? How do we find Miss Draper and bring her back with us?"

"It's just a small mining planet. There won't be any guards or security. So we just have a look around, it shouldn't be too difficult to find her, get her on the ship and return home as heroes."

Maffee wasn't at all convinced by Chuttle's plan, but he didn't have any better ideas.

"How long before we reach Suvmar?"

"A couple of days maximum. So just relax and take it easy, there'll be plenty of time for action pretty soon."

Chapter Nine

Professor Saffa, the grey bearded scientist that Blista had been shouting at, walked into the room where Mo Draper was being held. This room was much different to the one that she had first woken up in. It was more like an office, brightly lit with a comfortable swivel chair and a large metal desk. A computer screen sat on the corner of the desk and some brown files and data sticks sat on the other corner. A large picture of Blista standing in front of a large white Earth building hung on the wall.

Saffa didn't bother with polite introductions.

"I want to see what progress you've made with the final designs and then I need you to come with me to the laboratory to check the first stages of the prototype we're building."

Mo was staring hard, trying to recall where she had seen the man in front of her before.

"You're Professor Seymour Saffa aren't you?"

"That's right."

"You worked for the InterEarth Government about fifteen years ago didn't you?"

"Yes I did. And it's a period of my life I've spent the last fifteen years trying not to think about." Saffa snapped back.

"Why? You were brilliant. I've watched all of your research files. You developed and built the very first Rusdan powered fighter craft and your work on sonar energy drives helped us to develop the tri-arm razor light. You were the most brilliant scientist in our solar system and then you just left for no reason."

Saffa turned to look at Mo, his eyes wide with indignation.

"No reason! Is that what they say? I had reason alright. The reason I left was because they made me leave, kicked me out and told me to leave Earth forever."

"Why would they do that?"

"Because, Miss Draper, your government couldn't understand what I was trying to do. I was trying to save lives, bring peace, but all they were interested in was how to win wars and conquer planets. They wouldn't draw a line between the ability to defend a planet and the ability to destroy one."

"What do you mean?"

"The Delta Brain project."

"The Delta Brain project? That's the basis of our planetary defence system. A system that has been sold to every other planet within the InterEarth government's union, to protect them all from any unexpected attack. The brain of the system can detect and automatically respond to a surprise attack before the enemy is even within striking distance by shutting down their weapons system. It's the perfect defence mechanism, avoiding any casualties on any side and no-one has managed to create a weapons system that can beat it. But what did you have to do with that project?"

"What did I have to do with it? I designed it. I built it." Saffa snapped angrily.

"If you designed it you should have been rewarded, not thrown out. Why would they do that?"

"Because like every other powerful government, race or individual in this Universe, your InterEarth government weren't satisfied with what they had. Instead they wanted more power and more control."

"Like your friend Blista." Mo interrupted.

Saffa realised he had been talking too much and changed the subject back to the JXX7.

"None of that matters now. What is important is that you get to work. The sooner you get this JXX7 built, the sooner you can leave this planet and see your family again."

Mo thought for a moment then said.

"That's why Blista wants the JXX7s isn't it. With the JXX7 he

55

can get past the Delta Brain defence systems and take control. And who better to advise him on the Delta Brain system than the man who designed it. I bet that's why you left Earth, to work for Blista instead. I hope Blista is paying you a lot for your help. Enough money to help you forget about the millions of people whose lives will be ruined if Blista takes over."

"What makes you think that Mr Blista wants anything different than what your government wants? They're both after more power, they both want to be able to control other people's lives and they don't care how they do it."

"And you obviously don't mind helping, so you are no better!"

Saffa thought for a moment and then said,

"I suppose you're right. Although there was a time when I did care. When your government wanted me to show them how to use the Delta Brain system as a weapon, I cared and so I said no and that's why I lost my job, my friends and my home."

"If you cared so much why are you working for Blista?" Mo interrupted.

"Because I spent two years without a job, scraping by while everyone else grew richer and more successful. I spent two years of my life wasting away, being shunned by people who used to respect me and I started to care a little less. Then Mr Blista offered me the chance to work for him, leading new and exciting projects so I took the job."

Saffa lowered his voice, then continued "And besides, back then I didn't know what he was really like, I thought he was just a very rich businessman with scientific curiosity. As I started to work with him I realised he was a lot more shall we say, dangerous, than that. But once you work for Mr Blista it's difficult to leave. My advice to you is to get the JXX7 finished as quickly as you can and maybe you'll have a chance of getting out of here."

"If you know what he's like, why don't you leave? Why not go to the InterEarth Government and tell them what he's doing?" Mo was whispering too.

Saffa laughed sarcastically, "Ha! Go to the government? They wouldn't let me get as far as Mars before they send out the atmosguards to pick me up and shoot me back out to space. I told you before they don't like me very much."

"I could come with you. I'd tell them you were telling the truth. Then they would have to listen." Mo was excited now. She was sure she could persuade Saffa to leave Blista and take her with him.

But Saffa replied, "First of all your Government wouldn't believe me. Secondly there's no way Mr Blista would let me get off this mine unless I was with his guards and thirdly, I'm really too old and tired to even try. If we get this JXX7 finished Blista won't need me anymore, then he'll send me away to one of his quiet little planets somewhere to spend the rest of my days in peace and perhaps even a little bit of luxury."

"What makes you think Blista will let you go once he's finished with you?" Mo said, growing more annoyed as she saw her chances of escape fading.

Saffa thought about this for a moment and in his own mind wondered about the answer to Mo's question, but out loud he said, "My dear, I have little else to hope for."

And with that he turned and walked out the door. Mo assumed that this meant the conversation was over and followed him out of her cell and back to the laboratory to continue working on the prototype.

Chapter Ten

Detective Lychee was back in his office at police headquarters. He was speaking into his v-mail unit.

"This is Lychee. Do you have them?"

The trooper on the screen was one of the drivers that had been chasing Chuttle and Maffee.

"No sir. They got to the space port and escaped."

"Well did you call the atmosguard to intercept them?" Lychee was angry.

"We did, but the suspects were in a Dragonfly and were gone before the atmosguard could get close."

"Alright, well put out an intergalactic bulletin to all atmosguards to be on the look out for them and then bring them back here."

Lychee snapped the lid shut on his v-mail unit. He shouted to the trooper who was sat at a desk in the larger, open plan office outside. The trooper immediately stopped working on his computer and walked quickly into Lychee's office.

"See if you can contact Maffee, then put the call through to me," Lychee ordered.

The trooper turned and went back to his seat to use his desktop v-mail.

About ten minutes later he knocked on Lychee's door and walked in. "Put the call through to me in here trooper."

"Sorry sir," the trooper replied. "I got through to Maffee once, but as soon as he saw me he told me to look for the real kidnappers and then hung up. But there's another call for you."

"Who is it?"

"She didn't say."

"OK, put it through to me." Lychee barked.

Lychee's desktop v-mail rang. When he pressed the receive button he recognised the dark-haired Ironian woman on screen.

"Detective Lychee, Mr Blista would like to speak to you."

"Put him on."

The image of the Ironian woman disappeared and was replaced by the dark face of Gelt Blista.

"Detective, how is your investigation going? Not too well I hope." Said Blista with a smirk.

"Couldn't be better. I've got everyone believing that the main suspect is Miss Draper's cleaner. And he's making himself look even guiltier by running away. All of our efforts are going into tracking him down. We've got every atmosguard looking out for him and his partner so as soon as they reach the atmosphere of any planet, we'll pick them up. Once we've got them, I'll spend a good few days interrogating them. By the time I've finished doing that, the trail to you will be stone cold and you'll have all the time you need with the Draper woman."

"Excellent! You're doing a good job Lychee. I'm pleased we're on the same side. Just make sure no-one suspects that I'm involved. Now, I must get back to my guest and make sure that she has everything she needs before I return to Brillon. Fortunately for her she has been sensible and agreed to work for me. It's now only a matter of time before the JXX7s are ready and then I'll have everything I need to take over Earth."

"And don't forget about me," Lychee interrupted. "I'm not doing this for nothing, I'm taking a big risk working for you."

"You will be well rewarded. Once I take over Earth, I will need reliable people to work for me. How does the job of Head of InterEarth Police Force sound to you?"

"It sounds just right Mr Blista, just perfect."

"Good. Then you go back to chasing the cleaner and I will

contact you again soon."

Lychee turned off his monitor and leaned back in his chair. He had never thought about being anything else other than a Detective, but things were changing and Head of IEPF would suit him just fine. All he had to do was keep the investigation headed in the wrong direction, which wouldn't be difficult. There was no reason for anyone to suspect that Gelt Blista was involved and with Maffee running, he looked like the perfect guilty suspect. It was strange, thought Lychee to himself, why was Maffee running away from the police and what was he doing with the Pervian bear in the Tremen Quarter? But robots were strange things that he didn't understand, so he let his mind turn back to the day that he would become the Head of IEPF.

Chapter Eleven

The battered Dragonfly glided through space, passing stars, planets and moons for two days.

"I thought you said we'd be there by now," said Maffee.

"Look," Chuttle said pointing out of the front window. "You see that large planet to the right?"

"Yes. Is that Suvmar?"

"No. But Suvmar is just behind there. You better strap in. It's time to put my plan into action."

Chuttle got out of his seat and took his gun out from inside his waistcoat.

"What's the gun for? What are you going to do?" Maffee said with panic rising in his voice.

"It's all part of the plan. We have to make the emergency landing look realistic. So I shoot out the engine's power feed to make it look like we're stranded in space."

"But we *will* be stranded in space if you shoot the engines."

"Relax man - not if we crash land on Suvmar. Then while the ship is getting fixed, we look for your boss. I've already explained this to you once."

"I know you explained it, but that doesn't mean I think it's a good idea."

Maffee followed Chuttle through to the rear end of the Dragonfly while they were speaking. As they walked, they passed rooms to either side of them with unmarked doors. The corridors of the ship were not brightly lit. There was a pathway of two red lightstrips along the floor and light-patches on the walls giving off enough light to help Maffee avoid tripping over the large amount of clutter lining the ship. There were spare mechanical parts, electrical components and even clothes lying everywhere. Maffee guessed that Chuttle didn't see tidiness and housework as a priority. Finally Maffee followed Chuttle through a doorway into the engine room.

Chuttle was looking at the panels around the room. Each was covered with different coloured small lights, switches and dials.

"Are you sure you know what you're doing?"

"Sure I'm sure. If I take out this power feed here," Chuttle was pointing to a small panel with his gun, "that will cripple the main power supply to the engines, but leave us with just enough reserve power to reach Suvmar. It's a foolproof plan."

He fired a single shot from his gun. There was a sizzling sound as the energy from his laser hit the panel. Then there was a flash as the panel burst into flames.

"Is that supposed to happen?" Maffee asked nervously.

"Not exactly. Now where do I keep the fire extinguishers?" Chuttle was looking around the room. "Pass me that extinguisher behind you."

Maffee handed the red extinguisher to Chuttle. He aimed it at the panel that was on fire and pressed the trigger. But nothing happened.

"Oh. It's not working. Hang on a minute. I'll see if I can find another one," Chuttle pushed passed Maffee who was watching the flames slowly move across the panel. The room began to fill with smoke.

Chuttle came running back into the engine room with two more extinguishers. He held one in each hand and pointed them at the flames. He pulled the triggers. A short burst of white powder came from each and then nothing.

"Come on sugar, give me some juice will you," Chuttle shook both extinguishers then aimed again. This time when he pulled the triggers one of the extinguishers continued to blow out its flame extinguishing powder. The flames began to die down until they were completely smothered in the powder.

"See, I told you there was nothing to worry about. Come on

let's get to Suvmar." Chuttle pushed past Maffee again and went back to his seat. Maffee followed.

By now they were coming around the side of the large planet and a much smaller reddish brown planet was coming into view.

"OK, it's time to make contact," Chuttle said as he strapped himself back into his pilot's seat. "Remember we have to look like we've got a real problem, so make sure you act like you're worried."

"I am worried!"

Chuttle ignored Maffee's remark and pressed a switch on the console in front of him. "This is light spacecraft FF297LJ calling planet Suvmar."

There was silence for a few seconds. Maffee looked at Chuttle, wondering what was meant to happen next. Then a voice came back to them through the ships speakers. "This is Suvmar. You are entering restricted space. State your business with Blista Enterprises."

"Suvmar, we have an emergency situation. Our engines are dying and we need to land immediately. Please advise us where to land."

"Negative. This is restricted space and a private planet. Unless you have business with Blista Enterprises you are ordered to leave immediately."

"Hey, have you got your earphones plugged in the right way. I said we have an engine problem and we can't go anywhere until it's fixed. Just let us land and get the problem fixed and we'll be away."

"Negative. This is restrictive space and if you do not change your course we will open fire. You have ten seconds to turn your ship around."

Maffee's mouth opened in amazement. He couldn't believe he was about to be shot at again. "I don't believe it, I don't believe it. What do we do now?"

"Chill out man. You've gotta be cool like Jackson. They're not going to shoot us when we've just told them we're out of power."

63

"So am I hearing things now because I thought he clearly said that if we don't turn around they would open fire?"

Chuttle ignored Maffee again. "Suvmar, we don't have power, we need to land."

The Dragonfly shook and the whole ship lit up brightly as a missile passed in front of their window and exploded to the side of them.

"Oh my word, get us out of here Chuttle, turn around!" Maffee was panicking. He was gripping his seat tightly and staring out of the front window looking for the next missile to come crashing into them.

"Smoking Joseph! I guess they meant it," Chuttle grabbed the controls and started to turn the Dragonfly away from Suvmar. "Ok, ok Suvmar, we're leaving, thanks for being so nice, I bet the tourist industry down there is just booming."

The Dragonfly slowly turned to face the direction they had come but instead of the smooth quiet hum, the engines were whining and droning. The lights inside began to flicker as they moved away from Suvmar.

"Oh." Said Chuttle.

"What's happening now? Have we been hit?" Maffee was still panicking.

"Well, yes and no."

"Yes and no? What do you mean? Try and talk sense for once, will you."

"Well they didn't hit us, but I did. We're losing power because I shot the power feeds. Only it must have done more damage than I planned. We seem to have lost the back-up engines too."

"So what does that mean? How do we get out of here?"

"It means we're stuck, but at least we're out of range from those Suvmar bandits. I can't believe they shot at us. I'll have to call the IBR."

"IBR. What's that?"

"Intergalactic Breakdown Recovery. They'll tow us back to wherever we need to go."

"And where's that."

"So many questions with you. For a super-smart guy you don't have many answers do you? It's obvious, we switch to Plan B. When you make a plan, you have to have a back-up. See, if you were a Space Detective, you'd know this. You can't cross the Universe fighting crime and cracking cases just willy-nilly. You have to use what's up here." Chuttle prodded Maffee's head with one of his large fingers.

"I'll have nothing left up there if you keep bashing me about!"

"The life of a crime fighter is a lonely life. You don't have anyone to support you so you have to rely on your brains and be ready for anything. Now, I better call the IBR. It's probably going to take them a day or so to reach us which will give me just enough time to fine-tune Plan B."

Chuttle made the call to the IBR. He was told that they had a recovery ship in a nearby sector that would reach him in just over two days. He was secretly pleased. He could use the two days to think of what they were going to do next, because he didn't actually have a Plan B. He had been sure his plan to crash land on Suvmar would work. But it hadn't and now they were floating around in space with nowhere to go. He was certain that Mo Draper was on Suvmar, but he didn't know how to get onto the planet. The only people that went there were workers from the planet Ircone and Blista's guards. There was no way that a big furry Pervian and a robot could pretend to be Irconian, nor would they get away with pretending to be Blista's guards. He had to think of another way onto the planet.

* * * * *

For the next two days Maffee plugged himself into the recharge socket. He'd had too much action in the past twenty-four hours. He switched off his v-mail unit to avoid anymore contact with Detective Lychee and he shut himself down to recharge and avoid having to listen to anymore of Chuttle's stories of action and adventure, which he guessed weren't true anyway.

He switched himself back on at the start of the third day. He walked over to his seat and looked out of the windows. He couldn't tell whether they had moved or not, space all looked the same to him, but he couldn't hear the engines running and he guessed that they were probably still stranded. He sat and watched the stars glimmering against the darkness of space.

Maffee jumped when Chuttle bounded back into the cockpit. "Heyyy! The Maffee-man is up! How're you feeling? I hope those batteries of yours are fully charged and ready to boogie-woogie!"

"Boogie-woogie?" Maffee repeated Chuttle's words and wished that he hadn't bothered to bring himself on-line.

"Sure man, Boogie-woogie. Shake your thing. Ready to put Plan B into operation," Chuttle explained.

"Ah Plan B. Tell me something first, does Plan B involve me being shot at?"

"No."

"And does Plan B involve me being arrested?"

"Of course not, no. Plan B is almost as good as Plan A."

"But Plan A didn't work and it almost got us killed."

"Did I say *almost* as good as Plan A, I meant better than Plan A. Sure, Plan B is a masterplan."

"So what does it involve?"

Chuttle put down the box he was carrying and sat down in his pilot seat next to Maffee. "Here's the plan. We go to the planet Brillon, where Blista has his headquarters and we pretend that we want to buy a mountain load of Rusdan. Then we tell him we want to see the mines before we buy the stuff. Blista will take us to the mines which are on Suvmar and once we're on the planet we can look for Miss Draper, rescue her and leave." Chuttle rushed the last part of his sentence but Maffee wasn't easily convinced.

"So we just rescue her and leave? You're right, it is as good as Plan A."

"Listen, Blista is a businessman. We'll offer to buy so much Rusdan that he won't be able to refuse the deal. After all, he has no reason to suspect anything. Then I'll tell him that we're very careful about quality, therefore we insist that our Chief Scientist, that will be you, personally inspects the mining and processing facilities on Suvmar. When we get to Suvmar we'll obviously be given a tour of the facilities, which will take a couple of days at least. So in the evening we slip out of our rooms and search the areas that Blista hasn't shown us because those will be the areas that he must be hiding the things he doesn't want us to see, like where he keeps his kidnap victims. We'll find Miss Draper and then hightail out of there to our ship. Once we're in the sky, they'll never catch us. So what do you think of the plan?"

Chuttle finished explaining his plan and did a triumphant spin in his chair turning full circle, coming back to face Maffee. Maffee was trying to picture Chuttle's plan. The way Chuttle described it, it did seem feasible that it might work and more importantly, Maffee didn't think that there was too much danger involved. The worst thing that could happen would be for Blista to decide he wasn't interested in their offer and they'd have to find another way onto the planet.

"Ok." Maffee agreed. "We'll try your plan."

"Great." Chuttle reached down and picked up the box he had been carrying. "We'll need these disguises if we're going to fool anyone."

Chapter Twelve

When the recovery ship finally arrived, the pilot asked Chuttle where they wanted to be taken to. He then used a Magna-Ray Coupling beam to pull the Dragonfly into the recovery container of his ship by fitting a receiving unit to the front of the Dragonfly and connecting to this with a ray of magnetic energy from the IBR ship.

The IBR ship was very slow compared to the Dragonfly and Chuttle told Maffee that it would probably take them about four days to reach the planet Brillon. Maffee complained and decided that if his life ever got back to normal and he went back to his cleaning job, he would spend his spare time working on a way to speed up space travel.

* * * * *

The atmosguard checked his radar screen again. A new vehicle was entering the planet's atmosphere. He pushed a button next to the radar and a mechanical voice said, "Engine identification DX912-R07V-3HHE. Recovery ship, owned by Intergalactic Breakdown Recovery. Pilot's name is Critchen Rang…"

"OK. That's enough," the atmosguard interrupted the readout. The radar system was designed to pick up any ship's engine signal as it passed through the atmosphere towards Brillon. Fortunately for Maffee and Chuttle, the Dragonfly's engines were switched off, as it was carried through space.

* * * * *

On the fourth day they arrived at the spaceport. Chuttle had already told the IBR pilot that they wanted to land at the Satifargo spaceport, which was the closest port to the headquarters of Blista Enterprises.

The IBR pilot met Chuttle and Maffee outside their ship.

"That'll be eleven hundred credits," he said, without bothering to make conversation.

Maffee ignored him, assuming that the pilot was talking to Chuttle.

"Just a minute," Chuttle said as he pulled Maffee a few yards away from the pilot. "Eleven hundred credits! That's space robbery, if you weren't wanted by the troopers I'd call them myself and have this guy arrested."

"Well there's no point arguing about it, just pay him and let's get going. We've wasted enough time drifting around the Universe as it is."

Chuttle didn't move. With his hands in his trouser pockets he said quietly "I don't have that sort of money."

"What! Well how are you going to pay him?"

"Shhh, keep your voice down. Haven't you got any money?"

"No. I don't!"

"But you work for the government, you must have some money."

"I'm a Mechanoid Android. I don't need money. I live in the building where I work, so I don't have to pay rent. I don't eat or drink and I don't need to go out anywhere. What would I do with money?"

"Well you could pay for emergencies like this for starters."

The pilot was watching them suspiciously. "Hey. Have you got my money? I haven't got all day, I've got another pick up to go to."

"What are you going to do then?" Maffee asked Chuttle.

"Leave it to me. I'll sort this out," Chuttle walked back to the pilot. "Listen. We've got a bit of a problem. We haven't actually got the money on us right now, we obviously weren't expecting to breakdown so far from here. But, we have a bit of business to attend to here on Brillon and then we'll have your money, so if you could just wait for a couple of hours, we'll be right back with the cash."

The pilot looked at Chuttle angrily. "I haven't got time to wait here even for a couple of minutes. I've got another pick up to go to and time is money. So you two clowns better come up with a way to settle this."

"I've got two hundred credits on me. How about if I give you that now and then send the rest to you as soon as we get it?" Chuttle added a friendly smile to try and win the deal.

"Do I look like I was born yesterday with a peanut for a brain, on a planet where they give the job of IBR pilot to the biggest idiot?"

Chuttle was tempted to say yes, but he decided it wouldn't be a good idea given their current situation. The pilot continued to speak.

"If you haven't got any cash, what about cargo? If you've got something of value on board I might be willing to take that instead."

"I've got a useless robot. All it can do is ask lots of questions and hide in cupboards."

Now it was Maffee's turn to stare angrily at Chuttle. The pilot didn't find Chuttle's comments funny either.

"If that's the way it is, I'll have to take your Dragonfly instead."

"Hey, wait a second. You can't do that."

"It's in the contract. If that's all you've got, that's what I take."

"Hot Smoking Joseph! What will I do without a ship? There's no way I'm letting you take it."

"Listen, it's the law. If you can't pay the fee, you lose your ship. If you don't want to take my word for it I'll call the troopers and maybe you'll believe them."

Chuttle knew he was beaten. He definitely didn't want the troopers involved and he didn't have any other way to pay the pilot.

"Go ahead and take her. I was going to buy a new ship today anyway," Chuttle lied.

Chuttle and Maffee watched as the pilot took off into space, towing the Dragonfly slowly behind him.

For once, Chuttle didn't have anything to say, he just stared at the Dragonfly as it went higher into the sky, until at last it disappeared from sight altogether. Instead it was Maffee who spoke first.

"If I may say so, you didn't handle that very well."

Chuttle slowly turned away from the sky and looked angrily at Maffee.

"I'm not in the mood for your opinion right now. I've had that ship for six years. We've been all over the Universe together. It's got me out of all sorts of trouble and got you away from the troopers. What good is a Space Detective who can't travel through space?"

Maffee felt sorry for Chuttle. He could see that the big bear was really upset. "Listen, once we find Miss Draper and get her back to Earth, the government will be so pleased they'll give you a brand new Dragonfly, one that isn't covered in dents and dirt."

"Do you think so?"

"Oh yes. I'm sure they will when they find out how much you've done to help Miss Draper. I'm sure there'll be a big reward waiting for you back home."

"Yeah, you're right. We'll have earned ourselves some major credits by the time this is over. There's bound to be some reward money or something. I'll get myself an even better spaceship. Come on! Time's a-wasting dude."

With that, Chuttle picked up the box that he had brought down from the Dragonfly and strode off.

Chapter Thirteen

Maffee looked up, up and up, but he still couldn't see the top of the black, glass building in front of him. He had never seen such a tall building. They had passed many sets of entrance doors as they walked around the building, but finally stopped when they came to a set of large doors with a gold frame. Next to the doors there was a plaque and on it was written the words "Blista Enterprises - Universal Headquarters" in gold letters.

Maffee was dressed in a white laboratory coat. He felt uncomfortable because he wasn't used to wearing any sort of clothing and also because he wasn't totally convinced that it was a good idea to actually be going into Blista's headquarters. He felt like a fly walking into a spider's web. Chuttle, on the other hand, was wallowing in his role. He wore a silver business suit, shiny white shoes and was carrying a white briefcase.

"Remember Maffee, leave the talking to me. You just confirm what I say and try to look like a scientist."

"I'm more than happy not to say a word. In fact, I could stay out here while you go inside if you'd prefer," Maffee said hopefully.

"No, no. I've already explained the plan to you, we both need to go up there to make it look more convincing."

Chuttle walked forward and the doors to the building opened automatically. Maffee followed him into the building. They walked across the large lobby area straight to the reception desk. Chuttle recognised the receptionist. It was the same woman who he had spoken to nine months ago. He hoped she wouldn't recognise him.

"Hey there. We're here to see Mr Blista."

The receptionist looked up. She smiled and answered politely. "Do you have an appointment with Mr Blista?"

"Not exactly. But we're here on business, important business, it could be worth a lot of money to you guys so we'd like to discuss it with Mr Blista."

"If you would like to take a seat over there, I'll contact Mr Blista's personal assistant."

"Sure thing," Chuttle said and then walked over to the large soft black chairs that the receptionist had pointed to. Maffee followed and they both sat down.

"See," said Chuttle. "So far so good. The plan-man is in control. Before you know it we'll be face to face with our man Blista."

"And his men in black cloaks!" Maffee said nervously.

"You've got to be cool like Jackson. That's why I'm doing the talking and you just have to come up with the boffin talk when I tell you."

"Fine. But I don't feel cool and I haven't got a clue who Jackson is. But then again I haven't understood half of the things you've said since we met."

"That's because, Maffee my friend, you don't talk the talk. I speak the language of the Universe. I can communicate with all kinds from all planets, whereas you only speak in fluent boffin. So you stick to that when I tell you and everything will go down like a hot Marsian brew on a frosty Neptune night."

"Excuse me gentlemen."

Chuttle stopped talking and they both looked up. In front of them stood a dark green Brevetar male, like the one from the Hardware store in the Treman Quarter. But this one was dressed in a smart business suit and was a lot taller than the nasty shopkeeper they had met before.

"I'm Michcov Servitor. I'm the Director of Sales for Blista Enterprises. I understand you have some business to discuss. Why don't you come up to my office?"

"I'm Chuttle Jackson and this is the Professor. We're here to talk with Mr Blista about our business," Chuttle replied, not getting out of his seat.

"Mr Blista is busy in a meeting right now. In the meantime

73

perhaps I can take the details from you and then see if Mr Blista can fit you in. Please, I'm sure you will find my office a much more comfortable place to talk."

Michcov smiled and waited for Chuttle and Maffee to get up from their seats. Then he turned and walked over to one of the seven lifts passed the receptionist's desk.

"This wasn't part of the plan," Maffee whispered to Chuttle behind Michcov's back.

"Don't worry. Just go with the flow. When this guy hears what I have to say, he'll take us to Blista quicker than you can blink your metal eyes."

A soft bell sounded as the lift doors opened. Two large figures in black cloaks and gold boots walked out of the lift. Maffee began to shake.

"That's them!" he whispered, "the ones who took Miss Draper."

"And there's probably another hundred that look just like them in this building. Stop looking for a cupboard to hide in and get in the lift." Chuttle whispered back.

"I wasn't going to hide. I'm just saying that they looked just like the ones from the other night."

"Man, they all look the same. No individual style, that's their problem. That's why I would never join Blista's organisation."

They followed Michcov into the lift. Maffee continued to stare at the two figures in black until the lift doors closed.

The lift stopped at the 129th floor. They followed Michcov into a large office. There was a dark green desk by the window, a set of armchairs in one corner and a round, shiny table in another corner.

Maffee guessed that Michcov must be a very important man in Blista Enterprises to have such an impressive office. The people he had met from the government didn't have anything as extravagant as this.

They all sat down around the table.

"Would you care for some Scortee? I have it imported from the finest Scortee fields on Mars. It's expensive but I think it's worth paying extra to get the best, don't you?"

"Quite right," replied Chuttle. "I only drink Scortee from Mars. Anything else is a waste."

Maffee doubted that the big bear had ever even tasted Scortee, but instead replied to Michcov "Not for me, thank you."

Michcov spoke to his auto-com. "Bring some refreshments for our guests please. Scortee for two and some of my Brevetar snacks. I'm sure that if you've tried Brevetar snacks before you will not say no to them now and if you haven't had them, I'm sure you will want to try some of our finest delicacies."

"Oh yes, I always make sure I pick some up whenever I'm passing Brevetar. It's too good to miss," Said Chuttle.

"Really? It's so good to meet someone who has been to my home planet. Do you go there on business or pleasure?"

"A bit of both. I often have to meet with the Chairman of the Bank of Brevetar to discuss gold shipments and I often stay on for a few days afterwards to enjoy the sights of the Prearne Centre or take a cruise along the River Tathemt. It's such a relaxing trip, especially in the Third Season. I remember a particular night when there was a double moon that lit the water so well you could see the Squishes swimming below."

Maffee was amazed that Chuttle seemed to know so much about Brevetar. It sounded like another of Chuttle's tall stories, particularly the part about selling gold to the national bank.

"You're making me home sick. I don't get back there as often as I'd like to," said Michcov.

The office door slid open and a small robot hovered into the office with a tray balanced on its back. When it reached the round table it stopped and four legs extended from underneath it, raising the robot up to the level of the table. Two arms came out from the sides of the robot and it slowly placed the tray onto the table. It lowered back towards the floor as its legs retracted, before turning and leaving the room.

Michcov poured a glass of the red liquid for Chuttle and for himself.

"So gentlemen, what did you want to discuss?"

Chuttle undid the buttons on his silver suit and rested his hands on his legs. "We're from the planet Shaman in Sector Nine, have you heard of it?"

"No, I'm afraid I haven't," Michcov answered.

Chuttle was pleased to hear this. "Well it's just a small planet, not particularly significant on the Universal scale, but we're hoping to change that. We have plans to develop technology and industry on the planet and start to trade across the Universe. We have some extremely good scientists working on some advanced projects. The Professor here is our top scientist and he can tell you more about the projects later. However, the reason we've come to Blista Enterprises is because in order to develop our industries, we need to convert our power sources. At the moment all of our power is still generated by solar-nuclear fuel. Obviously this is very inefficient compared to Rusdan technology, but I don't need to tell you that."

"Of course not, Mr Jackson. Rusdan is the most efficient fuel ever developed."

"Please call me Chuttle," Chuttle smiled and then continued. "Our government is willing to make a substantial investment in order to change from solar-nuclear power to Rusdan generators for the whole planet. This means we would require a whole heap of Rusdan from your mines, plus we would want Blista Enterprises to build the Rusdan power plants on our planet."

Michcov's eyes had lit up at the thought of such a large order. "So, what sort of quantities of Rusdan did you have in mind and how many power plants?"

Chuttle turned to Maffee and said "The Professor will be able to give you a rough idea, without going into too much detail at this stage. Professor?"

Maffee shifted uncomfortably in his seat. After Chuttle had told him the plan while they were on the Dragonfly, he had done some research on Rusdan as a power supply.

"We estimate that we would need about two hundred major power plants and then three thousand minor distribution plants. Obviously we would need the appropriate amount of Rusdan for this number of plants." Maffee stopped talking. He didn't want to talk for any longer than was necessary.

"That is a large order," said Michcov, and he took a drink from his glass. "Tell me, how would you expect to pay for such a large contract?"

"Gold. A large proportion of our planet is made of gold. Therefore we have large gold mines which are our main source of income. I assume you would be willing to accept payment in gold?"

Maffee was staring at Chuttle in disbelief. He wondered how much more fantastic his stories could get. Gold was one of the rarest minerals in the Universe. All of the goldmines on Earth ran dry centuries ago and very few other planets had any gold.

"I'm sure we could arrange for payment in gold for such an order," Michcov said rubbing his hands together.

"Exactly. So you can understand why we would like to deal directly with Mr Blista. It's a business thing, you know? We need to know that we're dealing with the right company."

"Of course, of course. I'm sure Mr Blista would feel the same way and want to personally make sure this project is handled completely to your satisfaction. Please wait here and I will see if he can see you now."

Michcov walked out of the office. Chuttle had a big grin on his face, satisfied that his plan was working well.

Chapter Fourteen

Mo Draper sat in front of the computer screen in the small office. There was only a chair, a table, a computer and a lamp in the room. The door was still locked with a guard on the other side. It wasn't much of an office, it was more like a prison cell.

Mo glared angrily at the computer and continued to give it instructions. She had been trying for over an hour to find a way of getting a message to someone to send her help. But no matter what she tried, she couldn't access any means of linking to an external system.

"Unable to complete operation. EHR link required," the computer said in a bland, toneless voice.

"Ohh!" Mo shouted in anger and frustration. She hit the desk hard and then rubbed her fist because it had hurt. She sat staring at the screen. Tears began to roll slowly down her face. For five days she had been either working on the designs for the JXX7 on the computer, or showing Saffa and his scientists how they should build the prototype in the large laboratory two floors up. If only she could access her mail system, but she knew that Blista would have made sure she couldn't do that.

Mo wiped the tears from her face and dabbed her eyes with a handkerchief. She had no choice but to get back to work. "Computer, get me files three-four section two and three-four section three."

"File three-four section three unavailable or no such file exists. Do you want to access another file?"

Mo stopped. "Yes! That's it!" she cried to herself. "If I can access the SWORD department files, then I should be able to access the internal mail system and get a message to someone."

"Do you want to access another file?" the computer repeated.

"Computer. No thank you."

Mo got up from her desk and walked over to the door. She thumped it twice with her fist. The door slid open to reveal a large guard, dressed in the usual black uniform and gold boots.

"Tell Saffa I need to see him immediately," she ordered.

"What for?" the guard asked.

"You wouldn't understand if I explained it to you, so just call Saffa now and tell him I need to speak to him urgently."

"He's busy. Get on with your work and I'll call him later."

"Call him now, or you can explain to Mr Blista that the project has been delayed because you wouldn't get me Saffa."

He grunted and closed the door.

A few minutes later the door slid open again and Saffa walked into Mo's room. She was sat at her computer pretending to read some printouts. She wasn't afraid of Saffa the way she was afraid of Gelt Blista. She had spent a lot of time with Saffa over the last few days and had realised that he wasn't a bad or evil person, he was just a scientist working for Blista and was too scared to leave. In a way, she felt sorry for him. Mo guessed that Blista wasn't the sort of employer who would actually let his staff leave.

"What did you need to talk to me about Miss Draper?"

"Not all of the files I need are here. You only have the files from my computer."

"Well what other files are there that you need?"

"I have some earlier research that is stored at SWORD. You'll have to let me onto the GalacticNet so that I can link to their system."

"What sort of fool do you think I am? I can't give you external access."

"I don't need any external access, except to SWORD. You can isolate the link so that I can only access the SWORD system. I still won't have access external mailing systems will I? It's either that or I have to start from scratch on the Differential Blitsen Co-ord Driver. That will add an extra two weeks to the design time. Can you spare two weeks?"

Mo knew that he couldn't.

"Yes alright. I'll arrange the link. But you better not be trying any funny business, we'll be monitoring your access."

"Fine."

Saffa walked out of the room and the door closed behind him. Mo smiled. At last something was going her way. Now all she had to do was hope that there was a way of accessing the SWORD's internal mailing system from the file access that Saffa was arranging for her. She waited for Saffa to arrange the link.

"External link established," the computer said in its flat voice.

"Computer, show me an overview map of the SWORD system."

The screen in front of Mo changed to a maze of lines and file directories. There were thousands of files. It would be impossible to find the one she needed.

"Computer, locate directory v-mail."

There was a few seconds silence before the computer replied "Unable to locate directory v-mail. Do you want to access another directory?"

"Oh bother. Computer, locate all directories containing the word mail."

Again Mo waited a few seconds while the computer carried out the command. A list of about thirty directories appeared on the screen. Mo studied them, one at a time.

"OK computer, access DRIBUT/CMAIL/ALL"

The screen changed again and a list of files appeared. Mo frowned, these weren't the internal mail files she needed. She ordered the computer to take her back to the previous screen of thirty directories and began to access each of them in turn.

When the computer accessed the final one, Mo groaned in

frustration. She still hadn't found the files that would let her into the internal mail system.

"Come on Mo, think," she said to herself. "Where else could the mailing system be? Find something in the system that links to all users."

"OK computer, access SWORDNET," this was the intranet system used by SWORD to display general information to all staff. Perhaps access to that system was linked somehow to the mailing addresses, which might mean that Mo could access the Mailing system that way.

Another page of directories linked by lines appeared.

"Computer, access Distribution."

The screen changed again. This looked more promising.

"Computer, access Community."

The screen changed again and Mo jumped off her chair with excitement.

"Yes! This is it. Computer access Internal Mail directory."

A long list of the v-mail addresses of all of the staff members in SWORD appeared on the screen. Mo was about to highlight all of the names and send her message when she stopped. Somehow Blista had found out about the JXX7 project. Perhaps someone in the SWORD organisation was leaking the information. She couldn't risk that person seeing a message from her and passing it on to Blista. The only one she knew she could trust was Maffee.

"Computer, select address for Maffee and record this message: Maffee it's me. I've been kidnapped by Gelt Blista but I'm not sure where. I think I'm in a mining facility somewhere. You have to get help. They're forcing me to help them build a fleet of JXX7s..."

Mo stopped as she heard the swoosh of the door, then she rushed to finish the message.

"Maffee get help. Quickly! End of message. Computer send."

Saffa walked into the room, but Mo ignored him and continued to talk to the computer.

"Computer download file Draper\DBCD\Bars11to14 then exit SWORD."

She turned to face Saffa and smiled. "All done. You can remove the link to SWORD now, safe in the knowledge that your project is back on track."

He looked at her suspiciously. "In that case you can stop what you're doing and come with me. We're ready for the next stage of construction on the prototype."

"Oh how exciting. I can't wait to see the mess your boys are making of the JXX7. Have they got the Cranius Head Frame on the right way now?"

"Yes," Saffa said abruptly. "We're making very good progress. Now come with me."

Saffa walked out of the room to the lift at the end of the corridor, followed by Mo, who was followed by the guard. They got out of the lift two floors above the room that Mo had been using as her office. This floor was very different from the dusty, bare walls of the lower floor. The walls were white and smooth. The floor was spotlessly clean. A sign in front of the lift instructed anyone entering this floor to pass through the Cleansing Sweeper. Saffa and Mo both walked forward past the sign. The guard stayed by the lift door. An automated voice instructed them to wait. They stood still as the hissing sound of the Cleansing Sweeper moved from in front of them, to behind them and back again.

"All clear," said the automated voice.

Saffa and Mo walked down the corridor until they came to a large double door.

"Professor T J Saffa. Access number 318V2X."

The double doors silently slid apart. Saffa and Mo walked into a large white room sparsely filled with computers on each of the three tables, some machinery on separate workbenches and about six other scientists. The first thing Mo had noticed about this room was that there were no guards in it. At the bottom end of the room was a glass partition. Beyond the partition Mo could see four more scientists working on the silver skeleton structure of the JXX7 prototype. The scientists were moving around the JXX7 like bees around a honey pot.

"We've placed the basic power units into the three positions specified in the Rusdan engine drawings. I need you to check that everything has been done correctly and that it is functioning as it should. Come through," Saffa said to Mo as he walked down the laboratory to the glass partition. He gave his voice identification again and the glass doors slid open allowing Mo and him to inspect the JXX7.

Mo moved to the back of the JXX7 where three large, circular Rusdan engines had been fitted. She spent almost an hour checking each one carefully. Although Rusdan itself was an extremely safe source of power, it also created a very powerful engine. If all of the connections weren't made properly, even the slightest leak of power could rip a spaceship apart in a tenth of a second.

"OK, raise it up, so I can look underneath it," Mo instructed.

One of the scientists flicked a switch to turn on the anti-gravity pad underneath the JXX7. The spaceship began to float rising to about six feet in the air. Mo walked underneath and slowly she too began to float. She allowed her body to rotate to a horizontal position as if she was lying on her back. This allowed her to look closely underneath the engines. Again, she took her time to make sure the work had been done properly. Finally she turned herself upright again and instructed the scientist to turn down the anti-gravity so that she could walk out from underneath the JXX7, back to where Saffa was watching her.

"You seem to have fitted the engine units properly and all of the connections to the power supplies and exhaust systems seem fine."

"Good," replied Saffa. "Then let's run an ignition test of the engines while you're here. If that's successful, my men can carry out the full engine tests and let you return to your work. Please run the tests for me Miss Draper," Saffa indicated with his hand for Mo to get into the temporary metal seat at the front of the JXX7.

Once she was sat in the seat she began to check all the dials and switches were positioned correctly. "It all seems fine here, are you ready for test?" Mo asked.

"Ready when you are," Saffa said as he and his scientists stood aside, eager to see the first ever ignition of a JXX7. This was a very exciting time for a scientist.

"OK, here goes. Switching on main head power distributors. Number one. Number two. Number three. Setting Rusdan injector system to three point four SIPW. Waiting for pressure. Checking SIPW gauge. All good. Running basic engine computer system check. Number one good. Number two good. Number three good. All good. Ready for ignition. Number one!"

Mo pressed the ignition button for engine number one. There was a quiet, short hum and then the engine whooshed into life. Not only were Rusdan engines very safe, but they were also very quiet compared to all types of previous engine power. Rusdan engines didn't produce much heat either, unlike most other forms of power. Therefore it was safe for observers to stand relatively close to the engines when they were in use.

"SIPW stable. Going for number two engine. Number two!" Mo pressed the ignition for the second engine and again there was a short hum, followed by a whoosh as the engine fired up. The scientists were all grinning with satisfaction. For them, this was more exciting than a firework display and the birth of their first-born son all in one go.

"Going for engine three. Number three!" Mo pressed the ignition button. Nothing happened. Engines one and two continued to run but there was no life from engine three. Mo checked the dials and computer readings.

"Trying again. Number three!" She pressed the button again, but there was no reaction from the engine. She turned off the other two engines.

"What's wrong with it?" Saffa shouted to Mo.

"It could be the connection between the Basic Diffuser and the Grated Exhaust Unit. Go round and check it hasn't been tightened to more than seven grades."

Saffa walked to the back of the JXX7 and looked closely at the connection Mo had mentioned.

"It's set to seven point five," he called out.

"Lower it to six point five," Mo instructed.

Saffa adjusted a small lever next to the connection. "OK. Try it now."

"Here goes. Number three!" Mo pressed the ignition and heard the hum. Saffa heard the hum too and realised he shouldn't be standing behind the engine. But it was too late, almost immediately the hum turned to a whoosh as the engine fired into life, blowing Saffa off his feet. He flew backwards through the air and crashed into one of the scientists who hadn't had time to move out of the way. They both continued to fall backwards and land with a heavy crash against the glass partition. They fell to the floor with a thud. The other scientist rushed over and helped Saffa to his feet. Mo switched off the engines and climbed coolly out of the JXX7.

"I guess that works now, or would you like to try it again?" She smiled as she spoke.

"You can get back to your office now and continue working. We'll start phase two of the building. The guard will make sure you get back to your office," Saffa said angrily while rubbing the back of his head.

"Only if you're sure you don't want anymore of my help. I don't mind staying, it's kind of fun with you guys," Mo continued to tease Saffa.

"No. Just get back to your work."

Mo walked out of the glass partition doors, which opened automatically from the inside, and headed back to the lift, smiling happily to herself all the way. She was sure that by now Maffee would have received her message and help would be on its way.

Chapter Fifteen

Maffee was stood with Chuttle in an even more impressive office than Michcov's. His internal mail alert beeped once. With a blink of an eye he sent a signal to switch it off, he didn't want to get into anymore trouble by answering calls in public like he had back on Earth.

He looked around at the impressive furniture, ornaments and pictures. There was a huge black desk that was actually floating in front of the glass wall. The desk had no legs and Maffee assumed that it must be using some sort of anti-gravitational power. He'd never seen anything like it in an office and he wondered what other gadgets and technology Blista must have. Behind the desk was a large black chair and behind the chair were two even larger guards. Maffee looked away from the guards quickly, they made him nervous. At either side of the desk there were two statues of some sort of animal or alien, carved from pure Rusdan rock. The statues were as big as a man, but Maffee didn't know what they were.

To his right there was a large wall screen unit that looked like it was showing the Blista Enterprise company film.

The wall on the left was filled with photographs of Gelt Blista posing with various dignitaries and celebrities from around the Galaxy. Chuttle walked over to the wall and pressed the frame of one of the photographs. The image changed to show a short movie clip of Blista presenting a cheque to two young aliens. Behind the aliens stood the President of Krantal, the largest underwater country on the planet Neptune.

Chuttle moved to the next photograph and pressed the frame again to watch the movie clip. This one contained images of Blista receiving a small statue from another important looking alien in a large hall filled with people all clapping at the award.

As if by prompt, the guards by the window both turned to look outside. Maffee and Chuttle both turned to see what was happening. They watched as the air behind the window began to shimmer. Then, at the top of the window they saw two feet descending, then legs, a body and finally the head of Gelt Blista appeared, hovering outside the window. The glass window slid open and Gelt Blista stepped inside. As the window closed behind him, the two guards helped him to remove the small pack that was strapped to his back.

"Wow. That's a cool thing you've got there," said Chuttle.

"It's a prototype anti-gravity flight pack, developed by Blista Enterprises. There's still some fine-tuning to be done, but it shouldn't be long before we're selling them to the general public. Of course, the ones we sell to the public will be a lot more limited than this one. They will only be capable of flight up to ten feet above ground level, we can't have millions of people flying at aircraft height can we. Just think of the havoc that would cause," Blista began to laugh at his own comment.

When Blista had finished laughing, Michcov cleared his throat and introduced Maffee and Chuttle to Blista.

Blista stared at Chuttle for a few seconds, making Chuttle feel very uncomfortable. "Is something wrong?" Chuttle asked.

"Have we met before? You look familiar?"

Immediately, Maffee was gripped by fear. He was sure things were about to go wrong and he could picture the glass window opening again as Blista's guards grabbed a hold of Chuttle and himself and tossed them out without the use of anti-gravity flight packs. But fortunately, Chuttle wasn't panicking. "Well I do get around a lot you know. And I can see from these pictures that you do too. Were you at the ambassador's ball on Worren Nine last month?"

"No. I couldn't make it."

"How about the award ceremony for Universal Technological Advance Developments at the British Museum on Earth?"

"Yes. I was there. I presented the award for the best student project."

"There you go then. You probably saw me there. The ceremonies themselves are painfully boring but they're an excellent networking opportunity for us. It's a chance to talk to people about the developments we're making on Shamorn, our planet and also to see what other technological advances are being made elsewhere that might help us to bring our planet more in line with the other technologically advanced worlds in the Universe. Which brings us to the reason why we've come to see you today."

"Ah yes. Michcov has told me about your plans to change the power source of your planet in order to assist your development plans."

"That's right. We've got big plans for development of industry and technology."

"What sort of developments?" Blista was always curious to find new technology that he could buy or steal.

"Oh lots of things. Some commercial enterprises as well as military advances and some stuff that I can't talk about, it's top secret. Between you and me, the project I'm most excited about is Time Travel," Chuttle whispered this last part of his story.

Maffee stared at Chuttle in disbelief, but Blista looked intrigued. "Really? I thought scientists had abandoned the possibility of time travel many years ago."

"Oh yes. Some scientists maybe, but on Shamorn, we've got some super-brains working on a new theory, isn't that right Professor?"

Maffee looked extremely uncomfortable at Chuttle's latest story. "Yes, but it's not a project I have anything to do with. I'm involved with arranging the supply of Rusdan to our planet remember."

"Well anyway, we've got a lot of projects going on, so the important thing is that we have a reliable and efficient power source."

"Well Rusdan is certainly that, as you surely already know?" Blista turned to look at Maffee as he said this.

"Er, yes, exactly. Rusdan…very efficient source, yes," Maffee wished that he'd never let Chuttle talk him into this. He was sure something was about to go wrong and they'd be taking the express elevator out of the building - straight through the window, they probably wouldn't even bother to open it first.

"So Mr Blista," Chuttle decided he had better say something before Maffee shook himself to pieces in front of their eyes. "Before we make such an investment it's important that we are happy with the quality of your products and for that we need to start by inspecting your mining operations."

"Hmm. I'm not sure that will be possible. You see the mine is on a very inhospitable planet. Conditions there might not be what you are used to. It's a wild planet and mining is a very harsh business so it's important we treat the employees in the right way in order to keep them loyal, if you know what I mean. However, I can assure you the quality of the product is our main concern."

"Don't worry about your methods for looking after your staff Mr Blista. It's the same on our planet, you have to take certain actions in order to keep the workers in line, so we're not bothered how you get, or keep your men, but we need to see how you mine and ensure you can meet our needs."

Blista thought for a moment then said, "Very well. I have to go back there tonight anyway so you can accompany me."

He paused and then added, "But be aware, I like to keep the details of my mining operations away from the attention of outsiders, so what you see is confidential. Any breach of that confidence will be dealt with appropriately," Blista glanced at his hooded guards and then back at Chuttle and Maffee as he said this.

"Great," said Chuttle. "When do we leave?"

"Now. I have to spend a couple of days at the mine, which will give you plenty of time to have a look around. Michcov will escort you up to the flight pad. I'll meet you there."

Blista headed back to the window that he had entered through.

"Hey, are you flying back up there with your back pack thing?" Chuttle asked.

"Yes. It's a real buzz."

"I don't suppose you've got a spare that would fit a Pervian like me?"

"Certainly. How about you Professor, would you care to join us?"

Maffee looked shocked at the thought of flying up the outside of the building using one of the flight packs. "I'd rather take the lift with Mr Michcov, thank you."

"OK, see you at the top."

Maffee followed Michcov out of the office and back into the executive lift. There was a slight jolt as the lift stopped on the 325th floor. When they stepped out of the lift Michcov took two oxygen inhalers from the guard on duty and offered one to Maffee. At 325 floors high, the air was very thin outside and most people required an oxygen inhaler to breath.

"Do you need one of these?"

"No thank you. I am not reliant on oxygen. I run purely on recyclable Rusdan."

"OK. Let's go then. I imagine Mr Blista and Chuttle are already up here."

Another automatic door slid open to let Michcov and Maffee out to the top of the Blista building. It was cooler outside but not as windy as Maffee had expected it to be.

"We have continuous air current restrictors around the building to allow our space craft to land more easily. It also means we don't get blown about when we're at this altitude," Michcov explained.

They walked around the side of the building. The first thing Maffee saw was a large, gleaming black space cruiser. The first thing he heard was Chuttle.

"Yee-hah! Oh yeah! This is out of sight. Coming in for landing!"

Maffee looked up to see Chuttle with an anti-gravitational flight pack swooping down towards him. Maffee put his hands up to protect himself but Chuttle stopped just inches away.

"Man, these things are great. You should have had a go Professor."

Maffee gave Chuttle a disapproving look and then carried on walking towards the space cruiser where Blista was waiting. Chuttle floated across to join them and then gently lowered himself to the ground to remove the flight pack.

"How long will it take to get to Suvmar in this beauty?" Chuttle asked.

"We should be there within a day. That should give you a chance to look around some of the facilities at the mine before joining me for dinner."

"Wow. Within a day. That's some speed. You must have a whole heap of engine packed at the back of this thing."

"Well, there's no point wasting time trying to get from A to B is there. We're busy beings and the quicker we get to where we need to be, the more time there is to do what we have to do. However, while we're travelling to Suvmar, we might as well relax. I'm sure you'll find my ship comfortable."

Blista pointed towards the door and Chuttle, Maffee and Blista boarded the ship that would take them to Suvmar.

Chapter Sixteen

Blista's space craft landed in a large cavern inside Suvmar. Maffee and Chuttle followed Blista out of the landing deck and towards a lift.

"The surface of this planet is very hostile," explained Blista as they walked. "There are howling winds and fierce storms every day. When it snows, it comes down so thickly that you can't see your own hand in front of your face and unless you find shelter quickly, you'll end up buried alive under snow that then freezes to ice before anyone has time to dig you out. And of course, you have to wear oxygen inhalers, as the air isn't breathable. We've had to build air systems throughout the inside of the mines."

"Hmm, nasty. I once spent my holiday in a place that felt like that," said Chuttle. "Just as we landed on the planet, the weather turned so bad that we couldn't go outside and couldn't take off again. A one week holiday turned into a three week nightmare. We might have been there longer but there was a short break in the cloud and I took the chance to blast off that rock."

"Well no-one comes here for a holiday. I guarantee you that," Blista replied.

"I'll bet," said Chuttle, as he and Maffee both thought back to when they had almost been shot out of space when they had first tried to land on the planet. "I bet you're not too keen on uninvited guests here."

Blista stared suspiciously at Chuttle. Maffee looked down at his feet nervously.

"I mean, a mine isn't the place for tourists. They'd only get in the way, right?"

"Quite right." Said Blista as he stepped into the lift. "Come, let me show you the heart of our Rusdan operation. After all, that's what you've come here for."

Maffee felt his feet lift slightly off the ground as the lift rushed downwards, deeper into the mines. It came to a gentle stop at floor forty-six.

"How far down are we anyway?" asked Chuttle.

"Put it this way, if you tried to climb up the stairs to get back up to ground level, it would take a highly trained athlete almost a full Earth hour."

"Wow. That's a lot of stairs."

"Actually, there are no stairs. Only lifts."

"So what if there's a power cut?"

"Look around you. You're on a planet that's made of Rusdan. Pure power."

"OK, you won't run out of energy. But what if something goes wrong with the power systems themselves?"

"It's essential that that doesn't happen obviously. I ensure my engineers check all the systems everyday. In our eleven years of mining on Suvmar, we've only lost power once. The engineer responsible on that day never made the same mistake again."

Blista's eyes narrowed as he made this last statement. Chuttle saw again the chilling face that he had seen the first time he saw Blista nine months ago. Maffee turned away, scared that if he continued to look at Blista's face he'd be reduced to a trembling wreck again.

"Now," Blista said, relaxing his tone. "The heart of the mine," and he walked out of the lift. They followed him to the huge open mine face with its web of tunnels, bridges, ladders, tracks and pathways.

Automated carts travelled down lightrails, their carriages almost overflowing with dark brown, raw rusdan. Hundreds of workers trudged wearily around the mines as fierce looking guards dressed in the standard black clothing and somewhat dusty, gold boots watched them all closely, making sure no-one stopped for an unscheduled rest or drink.

Blista led them around the mine, showing them how the

94

tunnels were blasted with clean precision by sonic based technology. Then how the workers would use primitive shovels to collect the rusdan rocks and transfer it into the carts. He explained that the carts then took the rusdan to another part of the mining facility where it was checked for purity by laser calibrated energy meters that Blista had designed himself. Any sub-standard rusdan was rejected so that all his customers could be certain that they were receiving only the purest of power cells.

The pure rusdan would then be reduced to powder in a huge crusher before being measured out and encased in the appropriately sized chrome tubes.

"Excuse me Mr Blista," although Maffee was extremely nervous his scientific curiosity had the better of him and he couldn't resist asking a question. "With all this technology at your disposal, why do the workers use old fashioned shovels to collect the rusdan rocks?"

"An excellent question, which can be answered in simple terms. It's economics. It would cost hundreds of thousands of credits to buy shovelling equipment and maintain it, whereas, on the other hand, these workers are very cheap and I have a large supply of them."

"But surely labour costs are expensive?" Maffee asked innocently. Unaware that the workers were slaves who were trapped in the mine and had no choice but to work for Blista.

"Believe me Professor, these workers are extremely reasonable. Which means that I can keep the cost of rusdan to a minimum for customers, like you," he smiled the same creepy smile which was enough to stop Maffee asking anymore questions.

"However, if you want to see technology at work, come with me and I'll show you the most advanced crushing machinery in the Universe. I had it designed by my own scientists. Follow me."

Blista led them back to the lift. Chuttle was watching Blista as he pressed the buttons for floor fifty four. He noticed that the lift panel was not unlike most multi-storey lift panels. It contained eleven buttons numbered from minus one to zero to nine, buttons for opening the doors and keeping them closed and buttons for clockwise and anti-clockwise travel, as well as an emergency stop and a speech control sensor for people, or beings, who couldn't operate buttons. However, this panel was slightly different and Chuttle thought that this difference could be an important clue in their search for Mo Draper.

"Say Mr Blista, why is button number three gold, and all the other buttons are black?"

Blista didn't answer straight away, as if he was choosing his words carefully. Then he said.

"You're very observant aren't you Mr Jackson? Floors thirty to thirty-nine are where all of my special projects are kept and my most advanced research takes place. A lot of it is extremely top secret and therefore general workers are forbidden access to those areas."

"You mean projects like those anti-gravity flight packs?"

"That's right. And as an extra precaution, the number three button can only be operated by inserting this key first," Blista pulled out a golden key from his inside jacket pocket.

But Chuttle still had questions.

"So what happens if a general worker needs to go to floor three, or any other floor with a three in it, like twenty three or fifty three?"

"Then they press the floor above the one they want such as floor four and then press the minus one button. Four minus one will get them to floor three."

"Oh. That makes sense I suppose. So can we see some of your special projects?"

"I'm afraid not. As I said, they are extremely top secret."

"OK. So are you working on anything as cool as the anti gravity packs? 'Cos they were really cool."

Blista paused again before answering with a slight smile on his face. "Well yes, I do have a few exciting projects in development. One of them in particular is extremely, cool, as you put it. In fact, I'd say it could even change the Universe."

Blista's last words made the fluids in Maffee's joints turn to ice. He felt himself begin to tremble as he remembered Mo's words: "If it fell into the wrong hands, the consequences could be disastrous for the whole Universe!"

He was now convinced more than ever, that Blista had kidnapped Mo Draper and that she was being held somewhere on Suvmar. He tried to let Chuttle know by discretely tugging the fur on the back of Chuttle's neck.

"Ouch! What did you do that for?" said Chuttle.

Blista turned around to see what was happening.

"Nothing, sorry," Maffee looked down at the floor again.

The lift doors opened and Blista walked ahead of them. This floor was much quieter than the mine face. They were in a wide corridor. It was as wide as a street back on Earth. There were lightrails running up and down the floor. These were used to guide the carts carrying the rusdan. Brown powder and clumps of rusdan that had fallen off the carts were scattered over the floor. Workers walked in different directions, carrying tools and papers while a few guards stood watching silently.

"So is this where the rock crushers are?" Asked Chuttle.

"That's right. They're just down this corridor," and they continued to walk.

"There's not much noise."

"No. As I said, they're very high-tech machines. The most advanced thing you'll find on my planet, at the moment," Blista's sickly smile slid across his greasy face as he thought about the fleet of JXX7's that would soon be ready.

Maffee was walking behind Blista and Chuttle. He pulled on Chuttle's jacket. Chuttle turned around.

"What's up with you?"

Maffee used a hand gesture to indicate to Chuttle to walk with him as he slowed down so that there was a bigger distance between Blista and themselves.

"It's him! He's definitely got Miss Draper and she's here, on this planet somewhere!" he whispered sharply.

"I know that. That's why we've come here. What's the matter, have you lost a few memory cells?"

"I know you said so, but I never really believed you. But now I'm sure she's here. He's got her and we've got to find her."

"Well that will teach you to stop doubting the mind of the Universe's greatest space detective."

"Is everything alright?" Blista said. He had stopped talking and was waiting outside a row of doors.

"Oh yes," said Chuttle. "We can't wait to see the rusdan crusher thing."

"In here," Blista said as he pressed a door panel. The double doors slid open and they walked in. Inside the room there was a row of a dozen huge glass containers. Each one as large as an average house. There were all-sorts of pipes, wires and machinery connected to the top of each container. The containers were being filled with rusdan rocks, fresh from the mines.

"Now watch there," Blista pointed to the end of one of the containers where a worker was operating various switches and buttons on a control panel. "See how the rocks are turned to powder by what I call Zaddo-rays."

"Zaddo-rays? I don't believe I've heard of Zaddo-rays," said Maffee who was sure that with his knowledge of science he would have heard of such a thing.

"No. You won't have heard of them. I discovered them myself in these laboratories. Zaddo-rays are created by a combination of sound and light. The sound has to be at a level so high that it becomes undetectable by the human ear, and the light is dense light that can only be created by burning concentrated rusdan, not electricity. When the light and sound are combined, they create a blue ray that can pass through solid objects. As it passes through the rusdan rock, it breaks up all elements of the rocks into microscopic particles and all you are left with is powder."

Maffee and Chuttle turned to the container that Blista had pointed to. It was full to the brim with rusdan rocks. The worker at the control panel pressed another button. They watched as what looked like two giant torches began to move slowly around the top of the container. As the torch-like things circled around, a blue light shone from them into the rocks. These were the Zaddo-rays. As the rays circled, they slowly lowered down the cylinders until they had shone through every piece of rusdan from the top to the bottom.

Both Maffee and Chuttle looked in amazement as Zaddo-rays caused each rock to disintegrate until it was fine powder.

"Wow," said Chuttle. "Do these Zaddo-rays turn everything to dust?"

"Oh yes," replied Blista. "Anything that the rays pass through ends up as powder. It has the same effect on the toughest metals, liquids and even people. In fact, it would make quite a powerful weapon, but the problem with Zaddo-rays is that they have to move slowly through the target and they don't have a long range. So the target would have to be standing still and very close, but we're working on overcoming those problems."

Maffee felt very weak all of a sudden. The thought of someone as evil as Blista owning a weapon that could destroy anything, and having JXX7s to travel anywhere, was too frightening to think about. He began to sway, then wobble and then had a robot faint. His systems shut down and he keeled over, landing with a crash on the hard floor.

Blista and Chuttle turned to see what had happened. Chuttle bent down and lifted Maffee's head.

"Hey buddy, what's happened? Are you ok?"

Maffee came back online. He spoke a little groggily.

"Er, yes, I'm fine. I think it's been a long day and my system needs to re-charge."

"Of course," said Blista. "My men will show you to your rooms. In the morning I'll show you the rest of the process and then we'll head back to Brillon and work out the details of your project."

As Maffee and Chuttle followed two guards, Chuttle whispered to Maffee.

"I hope your systems don't really need charging. We've got just one night to search this place and find Mo Draper!"

Chapter Seventeen

Saffa stood nervously in Blista's office. It wasn't as big as his office on Brillon, but the one thing it did have in common was the large number of photographs of Blista on the walls.

"Sit." Barked Blista pointing to a silver metal chair across from his desk.

Saffa placed his hands on the cold metal and slowly lowered himself down into the seat. He sat stiffly, partly due to the coldness of the chair and partly because his body always tensed when he had to talk to his boss. Even on occasions like this when he couldn't think of a reason why Blista might be angry with him, he was still nervous. But this time Blista didn't seem angry. Instead he spoke quite calmly.

"You know you're trouble Saffa? You're a wimp. No backbone. You don't stand up for yourself. Look at me, do you think I got where I am today by letting people walk all over me? Of course not. I take control, I call the shots. I do whatever it takes to get what I want and if that means that people get upset, or left behind along the way, I don't care. It's up to them to look after themselves. And if they don't like it they can leave."

He paused to look at something on his computer. Saffa sat still with his hands clasped on his lap, still expecting the full force of Blista's temper at any moment. But when Blista was ready he continued to talk in a calm voice, much like a parent trying to explain something to a child.

"The reason you're here today, is because you let the InterEarth Government treat you like a worthless pigeon. And now you work for me and I treat you like a worthless pigeon, but you put up with it. I order you around, shout at you, make you do whatever I say and you never complain or disagree with me. And that's why you'll never get far in life, you'll always be at the bottom of the pile, looking up to people like me.

"I see. Well when you put it like that I suppose you're right." sighed Saffa.

"Exactly." Said Blista as he continued to work on his

computer.

Saffa thought for a moment then said, "Mr Blista, did you mean what you said in that very helpful and impressive speech?"

"Of course." Replied Blista. Then he added, "Did I mean what?"

"What you said about if someone working for you doesn't like it, they can leave. Is that true?"

"Yes of course. If someone wasn't happy, why would I make them stay?"

"So," Saffa spoke carefully now, "If for example, I perhaps, because I've been here a long time, and because I'm getting older and I've worked hard all my life, and I think I've done some really good work for you..."

"Saffa, what are you rambling about? Get to the point man!"

"Well I was just thinking that if I wanted to perhaps retire soon, not straight away, but just when it's convenient to you, perhaps after we've finished building the JXX7, then maybe I could retire. I've thought about doing some travelling you see, or perhaps taking up a hobby..."

Saffa stopped talking. Blista had a fixed stare and Saffa didn't think this was a good sign. Finally, after what seemed to Saffa like an unnecessarily long pause, Blista spoke.

"Ah Saffa my loyal friend. Of course you should retire if you want to." A sickly smile spread across Blista's face, a false smile. Then he continued.

"Of course I would be disappointed, but you can't be expected to work forever can you?"

"No. That's what I was thinking."

"And if you think the time is right to do so, then I welcome your brave decision. But you know, most people who work for me here at the mine tend to stay with me for a long time and usually remain in my employ until the day they sadly pass away. I think it's because we are like a family here and I am like a father to you all. I was hoping that you would do the same, and never want to leave. But if you've made your mind up about it I won't stand in your way. In fact, as soon as you've completed the JXX7 I'll instruct my best pilot to have my own personal cruiser ready to take you to a very peaceful planet that I happen to own. It's in a remote corner of space, far from any other planet and there's hardly anyone else living there, so you'll have plenty of peace and quiet to spend the rest of your days. It's the planet Buccie, have you heard of it?"

Saffa's heart sank quicker than a stolen space truck dumped in the Euro Sea. "The ice planet." He said quietly.

"That's the one! They say that during a good summer the temperature can get up to as warm as minus 90 degrees. Of course nothing can grow or survive on the planet's surface except lots of ice. Apparently it's so cold on Buccie that even the penguins wear thermals." Blista laughed heartily at his own joke.

"But don't worry, you'll have a nice warm underground house and a supply ship comes once in a while to provide food and drink to you and the other staff who decided they didn't want to work for me anymore. You'll be able to spend the rest of your days never having to worry about the heat wilting your pansies. So when do you think you will be ready to leave?"

Saffa looked away and didn't answer.

"Perhaps you've changed your mind for some reason." Blista said smugly. "I'll let you think about it and if you decide you still want to leave, just let me know. Was there anything else?"

Saffa slumped in his seat. He realised he had been foolish to think that Blista would ever let him leave. He stared at the crystal clock on the wall watching the time ticking by and wondered how much more time he would have to spend being shouted at and bullied. It seemed so unfair to him that his life had ended up this way. Then his mind wandered to Mo Draper, she was so young, it was horrible to think of her spending the rest of her life stuck on this planet, working for Blista.

"Is there anything else?" Blista's voice interrupted Saffa's thoughts.

"What about Mo Draper, are you going to let her go when the project has finished?"

"Now why would I do that?" Blista said as he continued working on his computer screen.

"You promised you would."

Blista stopped what he was doing and turned to face Saffa, "Promised! My mother promised me a puppy every year and I waited and waited but it never came. Promises aren't made for keeping Saffa, they are used to get people to do what you want them to do. And besides which, her brain is far too good to let go. Who knows what else she could do for me. No, she must definitely stay with me, you two will make an excellent team."

"I think you should let her go." Saffa said in a moment of recklessness.

Blista looked up at Saffa and spoke very threateningly, "And I think you should go back to work before I put both you and Miss Draper on a cruiser to that frozen planet we were talking about."

Chapter Eighteen

Maffee was in the room that the guards had shown him to. He was sitting on the edge of the bed. He had recovered from his faint and was not really sure what to do next when there was a knock at the door. He walked over to it and pressed the door pad revealing Chuttle waiting outside.

"The coast is clear. The guards have gone and as far as Blista knows we're catching some sleep time until the morning, so we've got the night to find Miss Draper and a way out of here. Come on."

Maffee walked nervously out of the safety of his room.

"What are we going to do?" he asked.

"Well, I figure that they're probably holding her on one of the restricted floors. So that's nine floors, thirty to thirty-nine."

"Actually, that's ten floors. You have to include thirty, plus nine more, that's ten floors." Maffee interrupted.

"OK, superbrain, ten floors is even better. That means we take five floors each."

"Five floors each! You mean we're not going to look together?" Maffee started to panic. He didn't like the idea of sneaking around Blista's top secret areas, but the thought of sneaking around on his own was even more frightening.

"We'll get the job done quicker if we split up."

"What if someone sees me?"

"Just say you got lost looking for the kitchen or something. That's what I usually do. I remember one time when I was delivering a package to the Sirepian colonies, I'd heard about their collection of rare minerals from some of the furthest galaxies. Minerals that they wouldn't let anyone else look at. The rumour around the worlds was that these minerals were the strangest and craziest of things. Some of them were supposed to be so bright, they could light up a building. Other types were supposed to be alive - can you believe that, a rock that was alive, it could breathe and move and talk, other rumours talked about minerals that could be turned into medicines to cure all types of illnesses, heal broken bones and even make people live longer. Man, I just had to see some of that for myself. So I started looking around one of their laboratory type places. The next thing I know there are alarms going off and I'm face to face with two huge guards. They asked me what I was doing. I said to them I was looking for the casino. They said there wasn't a casino. I said that's a shame 'cos I had some spare credits and was feeling lucky. So anyway, they grabbed my arms and marched me out of there. I thought they were taking me to a prison or something, but no, they took me to this small room where there were a bunch of other guards all sat round a table playing Sirepian cards. I must have been lucky that night. I'd never played the game before but I ended up winning big time. Unfortunately they weren't very good losers and didn't like losing their credits to a Pervian bear. They called me a cheat. I mean, come on, how could I cheat when I didn't even know the rules? So to cut a long story short, they took all their credits back, then took all my credits and threw me in jail for a week."

Chuttle thought about this for a moment before realising that his story probably wouldn't make Maffee feel any better.

"Maybe the ending to that story could have been a bit better. But don't worry about it, just pretend you're lost and you'll be fine. No offence, but no-one is going to believe you're up to no good. You don't look the type."

"Well I'm still not sure."

"Ok. Well put it this way then. Your boss is in this trouble because you were too scared to do anything. Now we've got just one night and one chance to fix this mess, are you going to lock yourself in another cupboard and do nothing, or are you going to put things right?"

Maffee was ashamed at the reminder of his cowardly behaviour. "I suppose you're right. But how are we going to get to the thirtieth floor, we need one of those keys."

"With this," Chuttle put his hand inside his jacket and pulled out a small yellow ball, the size of a marble. "Follow me."

Chuttle walked back to the lift. They went back to the floor where the zaddo-ray, rock crushing machines were located. When they stepped out of the lift there were still workers going back and forwards, carts carrying rocks and a few guards.

"Quick this way," Chuttle said and instead of walking down the main corridor to the rock crushing room, they went down a smaller corridor. It was much quieter and there were less people here. After walking for just a few minutes, they saw a guard walking towards them.

"Now just act cool and leave this to me," Chuttle whispered to Maffee as they got closer to the guard.

"Hey there. I wonder if you can help us, we seem to be lost,"

The guard looked at them suspiciously, "You shouldn't be here unaccompanied. I'll show you back to your rooms."

"Thank you. But before you do, would you take a look at this," Chuttle held the small yellow ball up to the face of the guard and squeezed it. A puff of yellow smoke drifted up from the ball.

"What's that?" asked the guard, getting angrier.

"It's supposed to knock you unconscious so that we can steal the lift key for floor three." Chuttle replied in a matter-of-fact way.

"Well, it didn't work did..." Before finishing his sentence, the guard dropped to the floor, unconscious.

Chuttle bent down and searched the guard for the key. He pulled it off the chain that was attached to the guard's belt and stood up. He sat the guard up against the wall. "He won't wake up until the morning."

"Someone will find him before then." Maffee said, worrying again.

"But they won't be able to wake him up, so they won't know what's happened which means we'll be ok until the morning. So let's not waste anymore time talking."

Chuttle turned around and walked back to the lift, with Maffee following.

Inside the lift, Chuttle took the golden key and inserted it into the golden number three button and turned it.

"It fits! Ok, I'll take you to the thirty-ninth floor and you start searching there. When you've searched thirty-nine, move up to thirty-eight, thirty-seven, thirty-six and thirty-five by pressing the minus one button. I'll start on floor thirty and work my way down to thirty-four using the key."

"What if you find Miss Draper? How will you let me know so that we can meet up?"

"Good thinking Maffee my man. You're beginning to think like a real crime-fighting space detective. It must be my influence," Chuttle reached into his jacket pockets again and pulled out two, small black pieces of plastic.

"We'll use these. It's an earpiece and microphone. Put it in your ear and we'll be able to contact each other."

"I don't have ears,"

"Oh yeah," said Chuttle studying Maffee's head. "Well how do you hear?"

"Through these sensors," Maffee pointed to the tiny holes at each side of his head, the place where ears would normally be on a human head.

"Here. There's a sticky pad on it," Chuttle peeled a thin piece of paper off the back of the earpiece and pressed it firmly against the side of Maffee's head. Then he took the other earpiece and pushed it into his own ear.

"There, can you hear me now?"

"Of course I can hear you, you're stood right next to me."

"I mean, can you hear me through the earpiece?"

"Yes, I suppose so."

"Good. When one of us finds Mo, we contact each other and arrange to meet up."

The lift stopped on the thirty-ninth floor.

"This is your stop. Now don't waste time, Mo needs us. So tonight, you're not a cleaner, you're not a boffin and you're not a chicken. It's time for you to be a crime fighter, a wrong righter, it's time to shake down crime and take out the grime. Now get out there."

The lift door opened. Maffee hesitated, then slowly stepped out of the lift, looking cautiously down the corridor and both left and right. He turned around.

"I'd feel better with some of those yellow sleep inducers, in case I run into any guards. Do you have any more?"

Chuttle rummaged inside his jacket, searching his many pockets.

"I don't think so. I was given them a long time ago. I think that was my last," he carried on checking his pockets. "Wait a minute, here's one."

He pulled out a faded yellow ball and gave it to Maffee. Chuttle then pushed a button and Maffee watched as the lift door closed. He was on his own now.

He began to walk slowly down the corridor. It was much narrower than the one they had been in before and reminded him a little bit of his old government office that he had worked in, except this building seemed a little colder and more sinister. He stopped when he came to a door on his left. "Ok Maffee. It's time to be a crime fighter," he repeated Chuttle's words to himself. He pressed the door panel and the door slid open. The room was dark inside. He guessed it was probably empty.

"I'd better go in and check," he thought to himself. He stepped inside the room and the door closed behind him. He switched his eyes to infra-red, allowing him to see clearly in the darkness. It was a large store cupboard of some sort. There were dozens of boxes piled up and rows of shelves of tools and equipment. A perfect place to hide, thought Maffee. A person could find a quiet corner in here behind a few boxes and not be seen by anyone. He walked across the room to a stack of large boxes and squeezed behind them.

"There. Safe at last," he thought to himself.

He stood motionless and quiet behind his wall of boxes for a long time. Eventually his mind began to wander. "What now? If I stay here forever, who will save Miss Draper? I can't expect that hairy, bumbling bear to manage by himself. He hasn't got the brains. He'll be caught and there'll be no-one to rescue Miss Draper. She will be forced to finish building the JXX7s for Blista and he'll take over the Earth, the galaxy or even the universe. And I'll still be here, hiding away in this store room, while Chuttle, Miss Draper, Peggy and everyone back at the SWORD team are all ruled by Blista's evil empire. Forced to do whatever he wants just like those poor workers in this mine. And all of that will be because of one stupid, cowardly mechanical android."

He shuffled out from behind the boxes. "Not this time. No more hiding until this is over."

He opened the storeroom door and without missing a step, turned left to continue walking down the corridor.

Some of the rooms he walked passed had windows, some had large glass doors. It was easy for him to see what was in these rooms. When he came to other rooms, he would have to open the doors. Although this made him more nervous, he would force himself to press the door panel. Inside most of the rooms were workers doing different jobs and sometimes guards watching them, but no-one seemed to take any notice of Maffee, which he was relieved about. He guessed that because it was night-time, there were less people around. This made it easier for him to move around unnoticed.

On the first two occasions that he was stopped by guards and asked what he was doing, they actually believed him when he nervously told them that he was looking for the kitchen. The guards pointed him in the right direction and carried on with what they were doing. This wasn't so dangerous after all, he thought. He continued to walk along corridors looking inside each room, but there was no sign of Mo Draper.

The third time that a guard stopped him, he didn't panic.

"What are you doing?" the guard asked gruffly.

"I'm looking for the kitchen," Maffee answered, expecting to be shown the way.

"You've just walked passed the kitchen."

"Oh, I didn't see it."

The guard looked at him suspiciously. "What are you doing on this floor anyway? Aren't you one of Mr Blista's visitors? You shouldn't be on the restricted floors. I'd better take you to see Mr Blista and find out what you're up to."

Maffee definitely didn't want that to happen. "Before you take me to see him, you should take a look at this," Maffee held the yellow ball in front of the guard's face and squeezed. His fingers squashed the ball, but there was no puff of yellow smoke.

"What's that?" asked the guard.

"It's supposed to knock you unconscious, any moment now."

The guard continued to stare angrily at Maffee and didn't look like he was about to fall to the floor. Instead he said,

"Right I've had enough of you. We're going to see Mr Blista," he reached forward and grabbed Maffee by the arm. Maffee let out a small shriek then pointed his right index finger at the guard's face. A jet of furniture polish came spraying out. The guard released his grip on Maffee and rubbed his eyes.

"My eyes!"

Maffee turned and began to run, but it wasn't long before he heard the guard's footsteps behind him.

"Chuttle, can you hear me? I need some help. Where are you

Chuttle?"

There was no reply from the earpiece. In his desperation, Maffee reached up to the side of his head and hit the earpiece. "Come on, work will you!"

"Maffee, is that you? What's going on, have you found her?"

"No, I haven't found her, but I've found a guard and if he catches me I'm going to end up as another ornament in Blista's office and you'll probably be used as a bathmat in his washroom."

"Where are you?"

"I'm on the thirty-ninth floor, heading back to the lift."

"What are you still doing on the thirty-ninth floor, that's where I left you? Did you fall asleep or something?"

"Never mind that, just get down here and help me."

"Stop right there!" the guard ordered. He was only a few steps away from Maffee now.

Maffee thought quickly. He knew he couldn't run fast enough to get away from the guard and he wasn't built for fighting. He had to slow the guard down. Without turning, he pointed his left and right index fingers towards the floor behind him and out came two bursts of carpet mousse, enough to cover a large area of the floor behind him.

The guard, who was running at full speed, didn't have time to stop before his feet were slipping out of control on the mousse. Before he could do anything, he was in the air then down with a crash, flat on his back. He lay on the floor for a few seconds, winded. Maffee kept on running without looking back. As soon as the guard got his breath back, he carefully stood up and began chasing Maffee again.

"Where are you Chuttle? Maffee called out. "He's catching up with me."

"Don't worry, I'm moving at greased up warp speed. I'll be with you any moment. Just keep heading back to the lift."

Maffee continued to run in his slow, robotic way. Every time he took a step he could feel the jolt vibrate through every joint of his body. He hadn't been built for running and he wondered how much damage it was doing to him. But then he stopped thinking about that and started worrying about how much damage Blista would do to him if he was caught.

At last Maffee saw the lift ahead of him, but there was no sign of Chuttle. As he ran past the lift he was sure he could feel the guard's breath on the back of his neck.

"I've got you now," called the guard as he reached out to grab Maffee. He didn't notice the lift doors open as he rushed past them, all he felt was a huge, furry shoulder hurl him sideways, into the wall where he collapsed in a heap.

"Shazam! Another one bites the dust!" Chuttle exclaimed, as he watched the guard land on the floor. "Good night, sleep tight, don't mess with Chuttle's might."

Maffee had heard the crash of the guard against the wall and turned to see Chuttle.

"It's about time, where have you been?"

"Where have I been? I've been searching three floors. You're still on the first one that I left you at. What have you been doing, hiding in a cupboard somewhere?" Chuttle joked.

"I've been looking too," Maffee said angrily. He was annoyed at Chuttle's accusation and even angrier because it was true.

"Well we better stick together from now on, before you get into anymore trouble. Let's get up to the next floor."

Chapter Nineteen

The double doors of the top secret lab slid open. Blista marched into the room followed by two of his guards.

The scientists in the lab looked up to see who had come in, then quickly looked back down at their work when they saw it was Blista. He walked through the lab towards the glass partition. Through it he could see the glistening engine of the first JXX7 attached to its skeletal structure. A slight smile spread from his lips as he thought of the power that would soon be his, once the fleet of JXX7s were complete. He could picture himself sat in the pilot's seat facing the leaders of the United Countries of Planet Earth and ordering them to kneel down before him.

"Mr Blista, I wasn't expecting to see you again tonight," Saffa interrupted Blista's thoughts. "Is everything alright?"

"As far as I'm concerned everything is very well. I hope you're going to tell me that all is well here too. What progress have you made?"

Saffa shuffled his feet nervously before speaking. Speaking to Blista always made him nervous, but speaking to Blista with bad news was even worse. "Well, we've had some minor setbacks, but we're making good progress now, as you can see. We've got the Rusdan engines functioning. The next major step is to fit the departicularisation unit, which is the unit that will turn the JXX7 and its occupants to minute particles and back again."

"And that Saffa, is the most important part. The part that will determine our success, our victory, our eventual rise to total power and control. To a position that no-one will be able to dispute or reclaim. But what is the delay? Why isn't it ready to test now!" he glared angrily at Saffa.

"Er, that Draper woman didn't have all of the files she needed on her computer, so we had to arrange a link-up to SWORD, to allow her to download them."

Blista's face turned red, then purple. "What! You gave her external access! I hope you watched absolutely everything she did?"

He asked with a threatening anger in his voice.

Saffa replied quickly. "Don't worry, I made sure that she only had access to SWORD mainframe and no other external systems. She couldn't have contacted anyone."

Blista didn't take his eyes off Saffa, not even to blink. "And what about SWORD internal mail, did you make sure she couldn't access that?"

Saffa suddenly felt sick. His stomach rolled over three times and he felt his legs go weak.

"No," he mumbled.

"I'll ask you again then. Did you watch absolutely everything she did?" Blista's voice was calm, but Saffa knew from experience that the calmness could turn to an eruption of deadly anger in an instant. All it would take was one wrong answer. Saffa's mouth was suddenly very dry. He couldn't speak.

Blista exploded as he guessed the answer. "You idiot! Get me a copy of that cunning woman's external access now. And you better pray that she didn't send any messages or you'll spend the rest of your life digging in the darkest, deepest part of the mine with your bare hands. I'll make sure you never see the sunlight, or any other light, ever again. Now get those transcripts!"

Saffa ran out of the lab, sweat pouring down his head and the tears of fear burning his eyes.

Blista turned and pushed the guards aside. "Right let's go visit Miss Draper."

Mo Draper was lying on her thin bed staring at the ceiling when the door slid open and Blista stomped in with his two guards.

"Don't you know how to knock?" she asked.

"I'm not here to swap clever remarks with you. I've just found out that my idiot chief scientist, who will soon be demoted to chief boot shiner, has been giving you access to the SWORD system. I hope it was only to retrieve files as you said, and not to try any funny business with internal mail."

Mo exaggerated a look of shock. "Internal mail? The thought didn't even cross my mind. What a pity."

"I knew it. You're lying. I want to know who you sent a message to. Tell me now or I'll make sure you're locked up in the deepest, darkest part of this mine forever and you'll never see sunlight, or any other light, again."

The two guards looked at each other and guessed that this was Blista's threat of the day.

"I told you, I didn't contact anyone," Mo said and went back to staring at the ceiling.

"Well it doesn't matter if you don't tell me. We have the transcript of your computer actions which will tell us exactly what you've been up to and then I'm sure I can offer whoever it is you've contacted something to make them forget your little message."

"Ok, let's pretend for a minute that I did send a message. The person I sent it to will have already received it, gone straight to the government, who will have immediately made sure that every member of the Intergalactic Space Force is on the way here right now. If I was you Mr Blista, I'd pack your bags and make a sharp exit while you still can."

Blista's face began to turn red again. He couldn't believe that his perfect plan was about to be ruined.

The door slid open again and Saffa rushed in with some papers in his hand.

"Well?" shouted Blista.

Saffa didn't know whether to cry, faint or head to the darkest part of the mine and start digging. Instead he forced himself to speak.

"She, she, she..."

"Spit it out you idiot!" Blista exclaimed impatiently.

"She sent a message to someone called Maffee, telling them that she had been kidnapped, erm, by you, and that she was held on one of your mines."

Saffa braced himself for the anger that he was sure to be heading his way. But Blista remained silent for several unbearable seconds. Then he tossed his head backwards and began to laugh and laugh some more. He laughed so loudly that the sound echoed around the room. Saffa stared at him, bemused by his reaction. He had expected to be immediately dragged away by Blista's guards, or even shot on the spot. He couldn't understand why Blista was laughing.

Eventually, Blista stopped laughing, but still with a smile on his face, he put an arm around Saffa's shoulders and pulled him to his side, then he turned to face Mo again, who was just as confused by Blista's reaction.

"Oh poor little Miss Draper. Did you think your cleaner would come to your rescue? Yes that's right, I know he's your cleaner. I also know that for some reason he's gone missing. Which is all very convenient for me because now your government, and the troopers, all believe that he is the number one suspect responsible for your kidnapping. And instead of looking for me, they're putting all their effort into finding your friend Maffee. So even if he does go to them with your message, I guarantee you they will call it a hoax and throw him in prison, giving us plenty of time to finish our little project. Isn't that marvellous?"

The sickly slimy smile spread across his face. Mo couldn't believe what he was saying. The message had been her only hope of being rescued. Surely Blista was lying she thought. After all, why would Maffee have gone missing?

"You're a liar!" she said. "You're in big trouble and you know it."

"Oh really? That explains why I'm shaking with fear and rushing to escape then, doesn't it. Oh, wait a minute, I'm not shaking at all am I, and I'm not rushing for the exit. Perhaps I'm not lying after all. Did you really think that my plans to conquer Earth could be spoilt by one internal v-mail to a cleaner? I think not."

He was right, Mo thought to herself. Why had she sent her only message to Maffee? He was a hopeless mechanoid, only fit for cleaning desks and washing floors. She felt the tears start to fill her eyes.

"Now back to matters at hand," continued Blista. "The facts are that I can still melt your parents' home down to nothing and I can still blow them off the face of the planet, if I want. But what I really want is my JXX7 finished and ready to launch by tomorrow morning. So why don't you tell me how close it is to being ready and then I'll leave you to get it finished," he turned to Saffa. "When is that departicularisation engine going to be fitted to the JXX7?"

"All we need is for Miss Draper to finish constructing it, and then we can fit the bodywork. But she seems to be taking a long time to do it," he stared at her angrily. She had got him into a lot of trouble with Blista and he wasn't going to forgive her. He decided he'd been too kind to her and from now on she'd do as he said, or else.

Blista looked at Mo again. "No more delays. I want everything in place by the morning. If it's not done, your precious family will be nothing but smoke and dust. Now get to work. Tomorrow I will get rid of my visitors and then come and watch the first tests of my completed JXX7."

Without waiting for a reply from either of them, he marched out of the door and headed back to his office. He sat down in a large chair behind a huge desk, switched on his monitor and spoke to the computer.

"Computer, dial Detective Lychee."

After a pause, Detective Lychee's face filled the monitor in front of Blista.

"So, Detective Lychee, what's happening on Earth, are they still looking for Mo Draper?"

"Well. She's not on the news anymore. But the government are still on my case. They're more desperate than ever to get her back. The longer she's away, the more likely it is that someone else is building a JXX7 and that's got them scared stiff. Every day, two or three times a day they ring me, wanting to know what's happening. Wanting to know if I've made any progress on the case."

"And have you?"

"I've got them convinced that the caretaker robot, Maffee is the guilty one. We're putting all our efforts into finding him. He hasn't been since the day Draper disappeared, he ran away from our troopers for some reason, so everyone thinks he's guilty. In fact I'm convinced he must have something to hide or why else would he stay hidden?"

"Well good. As long as they think it's him, they won't think it's me. I've got too much going on to worry about troopers as well. The first JXX7 is nearly complete. Once that's ready, I can start mass production without the need for Miss Draper anymore. She'll have an accident involving Zaddo-rays and once she's dust, no-one will ever find her and no-one will ever know it was anything to do with me. Until it's too late. But I need you to make sure they stay well away from me until the moment I launch my attack. Do you think your men are likely to find the cleaner soon?"

"There's been no sign of him since he left Earth eleven days ago. You wouldn't have thought it would be so difficult to find a pale blue robot who's travelling with an orange and black Pervian bear would you? Sometimes I despair of today's Troopers, I'll be pleased when you take over this planet and I can run the Trooper force the way I want."

Blista was stunned into silence.

"Are you ok Mr Blista?" Lychee asked as he saw Blista's confused expression on his monitor.

Blista recovered enough to ask slowly. "Repeat what you just said."

"I'll be pleased when you take over, so that I can run the Troopers the way I want."

"No, before that. Describe to me who you are looking for."

"We're looking for Maffee, the pale blue robot and some

Pervian bear that he's teamed up with."

Blista smiled to himself. "I don't believe it. What a lovely turn of events. Well Lychee, I think you had better fly here as fast as you can. You're about to make your government bosses very happy."

"What do you mean?"

"From the very distinct description that you have just given me, it appears that our two wanted characters have decided to launch their own rescue attempt. Maffee and his Pervian friend are currently asleep in the guest quarters of my mine. They're pretending to be businessmen from somewhere or the other, obviously in a bid to find Miss Draper."

"Are you sure? How could they have known that you've got her on the mine, or that you have anything to do with her kidnapping?"

"I don't know. But you had better get here as soon as you can, so that you can identify them. If it is Maffee then you can arrest them both and take them back to Earth for some very slow questioning. In the meantime, I'd better get my guards to check that they are in their quarters and not snooping around the mine looking for that Draper woman. Chop-chop Detective, you've got some police work to take care of."

Blista switched off his monitor and walked out of his office where his two guards were standing. "You two, alert the guards to check the rooms of our two visitors. If they're not in their rooms, sound the alarm and get them caught and thrown into one of the prison cells until I'm ready to see them."

Chapter Twenty

"All stations alert, all stations alert. Locate and capture Maffee, a pale blue robot and Chuttle, a Pervian bear wearing a silver suit. This is a priority order."

Wowoo, wowoo... a loud siren began to sound.

Maffee and Chuttle stopped in their tracks and looked at each other after hearing the message over the tannoy throughout the mine.

"Smoking Joseph! I guess they've realised who we are. How could they have done that?" said Chuttle.

"Well this is one of your plans isn't it? We were foolish to believe it might actually work. Let's face it, every idea you've had and every place you've taken me since we met has got us into trouble and almost killed. Why should this plan be any different? I can't believe I let you talk me into coming here, into the lion's den. Oh we're finished now, finished!"

"Hey. Snap out of it drama queen. Our ship isn't sunk yet. You need to stop being so negative. We still hold all the cards."

"Cards, what cards? I'm being negative because I happen to think that when I'm on a planet full of armed guards who are looking for me, there aren't many good things that can come from it."

"Look, we haven't been caught yet have we, so that's a good thing. Secondly, they don't know where we are, so if we keep moving and act smart we can avoid being captured. That should give us enough time to find Miss Draper and get off this planet. See, all positive with a happy ending."

"And what about the security sensors?"

"The what?"

"Security sensors. The sensors that can pick up the individual thought waves of everyone and identify who they are by comparing them with the thought records they have stored on personnel files for all workers on the mine. It's a standard measure for any high security facility and I've seen them all over this mine."

Chuttle thought about this for a while and then said,

"A-ha, but they won't have our thought waves on file, so they won't know it's us."

"Yes but they have everyone else's waves on file so as soon as they see the two that don't match any of those on file, they'll know it is us."

"Oh."

"So what's your great plan to get us out of this mess that you've got me into?"

"The plan is, the plan is..."

Maffee glared at Chuttle, waiting for an answer, but Chuttle couldn't think of one, so instead he said.

"Say, how come it's always up to me to think of a plan. You're the one who's supposed to have the multi-million brain, why don't you think of something for a change?"

"Yes I have a brain. But my brain is for things that you don't understand, like common sense. My brain tells me not to go with dangerous mad men to their planet without any way of escaping. My brain would have said that two people against an army of guards is probably not an even match so I should think of a different plan. But oh no, not you. With you it's act first and think never!"

"Hey, that's not fair. I found out who had kidnapped Mo, I found out where she was being held, I came up with the plan to get us here and now we're within walking distance of finding her."

"Ignoring the fact that there are over 100 guards looking for us and our every move can be tracked by sensors, what happens when we do find her, we still have to get off this planet."

"That's the easy part. We just head back up to the space port, get into one of Blista's ships and blast off out of here, back to Earth and a hero's welcome."

Maffee frowned at Chuttle. It didn't sound so easy to him, but he was trapped on Suvmar now and had to hope that Chuttle could get them all home safely. So Maffee decided to be confident and positive.

"Ok. The first thing we'll have to do is find Miss Draper then."

"No not quite," said Chuttle who was looking over Maffee's shoulder. "The first thing we'd better do is run."

Maffee turned around to see what Chuttle was looking at. At the far end of the corridor, he saw at least ten guards running towards them with weapons raised.

"Come on," Chuttle grabbed Maffee's arm and turned to run the opposite way only to be faced by another dozen guards running around the corner of the other end of the corridor.

"What do we do now?" cried Maffee.

"Quick in here," Chuttle took a couple of steps to the nearest room and pushed on the door pad. He pulled Maffee into the room closing the door behind them.

The room was dark but filled with thousands of tiny lights, buzzing around the room, like thousands of fireflies. In the dim light that they generated Chuttle could see rows and rows of computer equipment from floor to ceiling and from wall to wall. Instead of wires connecting the equipment there were the tiny flying lights, flitting from one piece of hardware to another, amazingly missing each other as they flew at dashing speed.

"What's this?" Chuttle asked Maffee.

"Shh! don't make a sound," Maffee whispered. "These are databugs. They act as connectors for central processing systems, connecting and transferring data, carrying information between the systems. Because of the high level of secure information they carry, they also have a high security defence mechanism."

But it was too late. At the sound of the voices in the room, all of the little lights stopped moving and turned towards Chuttle and Maffee. Chuttle and Maffee stared back, not sure what to expect.

"What are they doing now?" Chuttle whispered.

123

"We could be in trouble. These things are all linked up to all the mines systems, that includes the security systems. So, they will therefore have been notified that we're being looked for. Look."

They watched as the white lights of the databugs simultaneously started to turn bright red. An angry red.

"Oh. That's not good," said Maffee.

"They don't look so bad. What harm can those little things do? Come on, let's see if there's another way out of this room."

Chuttle took a step forward, but as soon as he did, the red lights came darting towards them both as if by command. Instinctively Chuttle began to swat at them with his huge paws, but there were too many of them, moving too fast. The databugs began to land on Chuttle and latch onto his fur. He was surprised at how heavy the tiny machines were. He tried to wipe them off his body and clothing but they had a firm grip.

At the same time, Maffee was yelling and screaming. The bugs were using some sort of magnetic device to attach to his metal body. More and more of them covered him from top to toe.

"How do you get these things off?" Chuttle tried to shout above Maffee's screaming.

"I don't know. How should I know? Just do something!"

There seemed to be no end of the databugs, more tiny red lights appeared in the room and flashed towards Chuttle and Maffee. They both tried frantically to pull and wipe the bugs off of their bodies but it was no good, there were too many and their grip was too strong. It wasn't long before Maffee was totally covered in bright, red lights. The weight of the tiny metal machines was too much for him to bear. His legs began to buckle and he dropped to his knees. Still unable to take the weight, he slowly toppled forward landing face down on the floor, unable to move.

It took longer for the bugs to cover Chuttle's huge body, but he knew it was only a matter of time before he too would be totally covered and helpless. He had to get out of the room. Straining under the weight of the hundreds of bugs that were already clinging to him, he turned back to the door that they had come through. He slowly lifted his heavy arm and pushed the door pad. The door slid open revealing the bright lights from the corridor and a large group of guards blocking the doorway, their weapons all trained on Chuttle. There was no escape this time.

"I'd put my hands up but they seem to be weighed down by these metal midges."

The guard at the front spoke into the intercom attached to his ear. Suddenly, all of the bugs released their grip on Chuttle and Maffee, their lights turned back from red to white and they flew back to the computer equipment.

"You can put your hands up now," the guard said.

Chuttle raised his arms in the air. Two other guards started to search him. They took away his 200 giga-hertz laser pistol, the solid beam rapier that he had been given by the Brevetar shopkeeper, three sonic flash grenades and a mini rapid stealth pistol.

Two more guards moved to where Maffee was lying on the floor and helped him to his feet. They searched his white coat for weapons but there was nothing to find.

"Come with us," said the first guard.

"Great," said Chuttle. "Are we off on another tour? Does this place have a games room? You know come to think of it, I'm a little tired now. It must be all this excitement. How about taking us back to our rooms so we can get some sleep?"

No-one replied to Chuttle's remarks. All he got was a prod in the back by a laser rifle.

"It doesn't look like we're guests of honour anymore Maffee. We might have to postpone our plans to return to Earth."

Maffee glared at Chuttle.

They were marched back to the lift. The guard pressed the buttons for floor forty-nine, the lowest floor on the planet. When the doors opened there was a rush of hot air that hit them like water from a hose. The corridor in front of them was dimly lit, its wall bare stone and rusdan. The guards pushed them forward and they began to walk down the rocky and uneven floor of the corridor.

At either side of them there were crudely made energy doors. These were shimmering doors made of pure energy. You could see through them, but you could also see their shimmering energy as they buzzed quietly. Anything that touched them would receive a painful shock.

Behind the energy doors were small, dark prison cells. Chuttle could just make out the hunched figures of prisoners lying on their hard, wooden beds with thin mattresses or sitting on the cold, stone floor. Who knows how long those poor souls had been there he thought.

"In there," said the guard, and he pushed Chuttle and Maffee towards an empty cell. "Get comfortable in your new home."

The other guards sniggered at their friend's comment, but Chuttle and Maffee didn't see the funny side. They walked into the cell. As soon as they were through the entrance doorway there was a click and the energy door buzzed into life. The guards turned to leave.

"How long are we going to be here?" asked Maffee.

The head guard turned around again to answer. "As long as Mr Blista wants you here."

"You can't do that. I demand to be released. Send Mr Blista down here immediately."

"Yes sir. Of course sir. We'll send him down to you right away," the guard turned and followed his men back to the lift.

"I should think so too. That Mr Blista has gone too far this time. I'll give him a piece of my mind when he gets here."

"He's not coming you simple cyborg. Not just because you ask him to. He'll make us sweat in here for a while; it may be a few days before we see him, if ever. Why should he care about us now? He's got Miss Draper, he'll have his JXX7's soon and as long as we're locked up he knows that no one will stop him."

"Oh my goodness. This is terrible, terrible," said Maffee, starting to panic.

"No my friend, it's perfect. Everything is going according to plan."

"What! Are you telling me you planned for this to happen?"

"It wasn't in the original plan, but you have to learn to adapt when you're living with danger everyday. I've adapted the original plan and now have an even better plan."

"Explain please." Maffee said, totally exasperated.

"We're locked in this prison cell on the forty-ninth floor, right?"

"Correct."

"So we can't do a thing to rescue Miss Draper, right?"

"Correct," answered Maffee, not knowing why Chuttle was bothering to state such obvious facts.

"So Blista doesn't have to worry about us anymore. He can just get on with his plans, right?"

"Exactly, but I don't see how that's perfect for anyone except for Blista."

"Of course you don't see it Maffee, because you don't have the mind of a super crime fighter. If you did, then you'd realise that as long as Blista thinks we're in here, he'll leave us alone. Which means that we're free to escape and find Miss Draper."

Maffee thought about this and then said, "There is a strange logic about your theory."

"I'll take that as a compliment."

"Just one question, how do we escape from this cell?"

127

"That's a matter of fine detail. I might need a bit more time to work that part out."

Chapter Twenty One

Mo heard the security announcement too. She couldn't believe that somehow Maffee had made his way to the mine. This was the same Maffee who had never in his whole lifetime been anywhere other than the government building and the local shop. She suddenly felt guilty for thinking that he had let her down. He had actually tracked her down and was now somewhere on this mine trying to rescue her. But why hadn't he gone straight to the police or the government for help, she thought. How did he think he would rescue her on his own? Perhaps he had contacted the government and they were on their way to Suvmar right now. Mo's heart lifted with hope.

"I'm pleased you've found something to smile about." Mo hadn't heard Saffa enter the room. "Well from now on you can forget about smiling and instead concentrate on working. You have caused me a lot of trouble so I'm not going to be so nice to you anymore. You heard what Mr Blista said, he wants the JXX7 ready for testing by morning and if it's not, you'll be in big trouble."

Saffa was still angry at being tricked by Mo into giving her access to SWORD internal mail. He was also still very upset after learning Blista would never let him leave the mine unless it was with a guard taking him to a desolate, frozen planet for the rest of his life. Once again he was being pushed around. Well he was going to prove that he was not such a softie, he decided that he had to be tougher and meaner with Mo. From now on, he thought to himself, he was going to be more like Mr Blista.

"Come on, we're going back to the lab to get this thing finished."

Saffa and a guard walked Mo back to the lab where the JXX7 was being built. The only people there now were three other scientists who were helping to put together the JXX7. All the other workers had finished for the night.

The guard stayed at the door while Mo, Saffa and the scientists set to work. Mo gave them instructions and together they began assembling and testing. All the time Mo's mind was on Maffee. She hoped he would find a way to rescue her. Any moment now, she thought, Maffee would somehow come into the lab, knock out the guard and the scientists and then get her out of there. Perhaps if she could get the JXX7 finished in time, they could escape in that.

At the back of her mind, she was also thinking about how ridiculous that idea sounded. Maffee wasn't the heroic sort. He was usually the one who needed rescuing. But he was her only chance to escape, so while she waited for him, she would concentrate on making sure the JXX7 was ready.

They were all engrossed in their work when the guard walked over to Saffa and pulled him to one side. The guard said something to Saffa, but they were too far away for Mo to hear.

"That's very good news," Saffa replied to the guard. "I must tell Miss Draper about this. I'm sure it will ruin any little plans she has. But when I tell her, I need the right smile, a smile like Mr Blista would use. How does this look?" Saffa grinned at the guard.

"You look like you need the toilet," said the guard.

Saffa changed his smile, trying to remember how Blista looked when things were going his way. He pursed his lips tightly closed and then tried to smile without showing his teeth.

"How's this," he tried to say without moving his lips.

"That's it," said the guard, secretly thinking that Saffa looked like some kind of strange alien fish.

Satisfied that he had the right look, Saffa turned around and walked back to where Mo was working. She stopped what she was doing to see what he wanted and saw the strange expression on his face. "Are you alright, do you need the toilet?" she asked him.

Saffa stopped trying to look like Blista and said in a smug voice. "I thought you might like to know that your cleaner and his friend have been captured and are now locked up in a cell at the bottom of the mine, where they will remain for a very long time. So, if you want to save your parents and yourself, your only hope is to get this finished before Mr Blista comes back in the morning."

Mo turned her back on Saffa and went back to work. She didn't want him to see how disappointed she was. Maffee was her last hope. She was sure that once the JXX7 was completed, Blista would have no more use for her, but he wasn't likely to just let her go back home either. She would either be held prisoner on the mine forever, or he would get rid of her permanently. She had to escape before morning.

Mo walked around to the cockpit of the JXX7 and moved close enough to float up and sit in the pilot's seat.

"What are you doing?" asked Saffa.

"I need to check that the rear synch drives work with the main ramhead operating. Don't worry, it won't take a second, but I'll need to simulate flight, so I'm shutting the cockpit hatch and sealing the ship."

"You're not getting into the ship now that it's nearly complete. I'm not stupid, I know as well as you do that you and the JXX7 could disappear with the flick of a switch now that it's operational."

"I'm not going anywhere, but we need to check the RSDs or Mr Blista could find himself in the middle of space, spinning like a g-ball in a game of Saturn Spelgoal."

Saffa thought about this then called the guard who was leaning on the door at the end of the room.

"Come down here. Stand here and if I say so you make sure you shoot her without damaging the ship. Understand?"

The guard drew his gun from his side and aimed it at Mo. The cockpit lid hissed quietly as it slowly closed. There was a thud as it finally locked shut.

"You worry too much Saffa," Mo said with a smile.

She began to speak orders to the ship's computer and press controls at the same time.

Saffa watched Mo closely. As he did he couldn't help feeling sorry for her. It was no good trying to be mean like Blista, he couldn't do it. All he saw was an innocent woman who was being bullied the way he had been bullied. Maybe Blista would change his mind and let her go after the JXX7s were built, maybe.

"I hope this works," Mo said to herself. Then out loud she said. "Computer, ensure all ship is sealed and auxiliary oxygen supply is operating. Good. Now prepare to discharge the NO13 gas chambers from engines one and three."

"Are you finished yet?" Saffa called up to her.

"No. It's going to take a while, I need to make some adjustments." Mo pretended to continue adjusting the controls in front and above her.

She kept her eyes on Saffa and the guard waiting for the right moment. One of the scientists called Saffa across to the back of the JXX7. Mo still waited. After more time passed, the guard became bored of pointing his gun at Mo and started to adjust the settings on it instead. This was her chance she thought.

"Computer, release one-third of NO13 gas from engines one and three now."

Saffa was talking to the scientist at the back of the ship when he started to smell something in the air. He looked up from what he was doing. "What's that smell? It's NO13. Guard…"

Before he could finish his sentence, every muscle in his body froze solid, even the expression on his face. The guard looked up as Saffa called to him, but he too froze exactly as he was before he had a chance to do anything.

Neldrotasium-Oxygen13, also known as NO13, was a gas used in the most modern spacecraft. It was combined with another gas, Hexorgen (HXN), to increase the speed of transfer of rusdan energy from the rusdan battery cells to the spacecraft combustion chambers. It gave them quicker acceleration and more efficient engines. However, a side effect of NO13 was that when released into the air, any person who came into contact with it would find their muscles, organs and even their brain cells frozen. They could not move, breath, see or think. However, scientists had found that the person was not actually dead and could be revived by submerging them in a simple solution of water, salt and magnesium.

"Switch off NO13 discharge and release 300 protars of oxygen, wait, better make that 400 protars, I want to make sure the air is clear." Mo then pressed a button to release the cockpit hatch. As the hatch lifted she breathed in cautiously. The air was clear, not even a hint of NO13.

She climbed out of the JXX7 and floated down to the ground. She walked over to the guard and took the gun from his hands. Then she stood in front of Saffa and smiled at his shocked expression.

"Don't worry Saffa. If I have my way, by the time Blista finds out about this it will be too late and you'll both be in prison somewhere where you'll have plenty of time to apologise to him for ruining his insane plans."

She turned to head towards the door but stopped as she heard Saffa trying to say something before his brain fully froze.

"Wait, wait Miss Draper," he managed to whisper.

Mo walked back to Saffa to hear what he wanted to say.

"Yes?" she asked.

"Good luck." With those last words he froze.

"Thank you." Mo whispered back and headed out the door.

If she had known where Maffee was being held, she would have used the JXX7 to escape, but instead she would have to search the mine on foot until she found him. Saffa had said something about Maffee being locked in the deepest part of the mine, so she decided to start by looking there. She walked cautiously back towards the lift, hoping that she wouldn't meet any guards.

Mo breathed a sigh of relief as she pressed the button to close the doors of the lift. Saffa had told her that the mine had forty-nine floors during one of her conversations with him as they walked from her prison cell to the laboratory. She pressed the button for the lowest level of the mine and then watched the floor numbers change as they were displayed on the panel above the buttons. She felt the lift slow down as it reached forty-nine.

The doors slid open. Mo looked out and saw a guard sat at a desk looking right back at her. He stood up from his seat.

"What are you doing down here?"

Mo had to think quickly. She couldn't afford to get caught again.

"There's been an accident. Someone's been shot!"

"What? Who?" Asked the bemused guard.

"You," Mo said as she raised the gun she was holding and fired at the guard. He was knocked back into his chair momentarily before sliding down onto the floor, unconscious.

Mo stood over him as she started to look at the controls on the desk. There were various buttons and panels, but she guessed that the energy door release buttons were the row of blue, red and green buttons, numbered from one to thirty. The blue buttons were marked "Camera". She pressed blue button number one and the visual display screen on the desk flicked to an image of a small, dark figure asleep on a thin bed. She pressed number two and saw another small, dark figure, asleep on a thin bed. As she pressed each button she saw almost the same picture each time until she started to think that each button was linked to the same camera in the same cell. But she kept trying each one. Then, when she pressed number thirty, instead of seeing a small, dark figure, she saw a very large, hairy bear-like beast. But that certainly wasn't Maffee.

"Oh Maffee, where are you?" She said out loud. She had looked in all of the cells and he wasn't in any of them. She didn't know where else on the mine Blista might have taken him. Perhaps Blista had taken Maffee to a cell near to where Mo's room had been. She turned to go back to the lift, but as she did, something on the screen caught her eye. The big bear creature was waving its arms and making gestures as if he was talking to someone. Mo looked more closely at the screen and there, in the corner of the cell she saw a skinny, pale blue, metal creature, Maffee!

She quickly pressed the green button for cell number thirty and then ran down the corridor. "Maffee! Maffee!" she called.

Maffee and Chuttle looked up.

"Who's that?" Chuttle asked Maffee.

"It's Miss Draper!" Maffee said, shocked at hearing her voice. "She's found us!"

"She's found us? We were supposed to be finding her. This is not cool, we're supposed to be the heroes, looking for the damsel in distress and instead, the damsel is the one busting us out of jail."

Maffee ignored Chuttle and ran out of the door. He looked and saw Mo running towards him.

"Miss Draper. I've been so worried about you. We've been looking for you since the day you were kidnapped. Are you alright? I would never have forgiven myself if you had been harmed in any way. Oh I can't believe it. We've finally found you. But how have you escaped, and how did you know we were here?"

"She didn't find us, we found her remember," Chuttle had followed Maffee out of the cell and was now stood behind Maffee. "Ok, so technically she might have found us. But we did all the rescue work. We are the ones who travelled hundreds of thousands of miles to get her and had to disguise ourselves in a daring masquerade and then run from an army of guards. So when they're telling this story in years to come, just remember, we are the ones who did the rescuing."

Mo was looking at Chuttle. Maffee realised she wouldn't know who Chuttle was.

"Miss Draper. This is Chuttle. He talks a lot and doesn't always make much sense. He has crazy plans and ideas that don't usually work, but if it wasn't for him I would never have got here."

"In that case, Chuttle, I owe you my thanks."

"Don't worry. I'm just doing my job as a crime fighter, a wrong righter. I shake down crime and take out the grime. Where evil is hiding, I come in riding. Where the bad dudes are staying, I come in

135

blazing. If you're no good brother, you better stay undercover..."

"He's a space detective!" Maffee shouted above Chuttle's voice. "And as I said, he likes to talk."

"Well we better start talking about how to get out of here," Mo said.

As they stood talking to each other, the guard slowly opened his eyes as the stun shot began to wear off. He heard three voices in the distance and looked up towards the end of the corridor where Mo, Maffee and Chuttle were standing. He grabbed hold of the edge of his desk and lifted himself up to his chair, still groggy from the stun shot. His hand reached out for the emergency alarm button and pushed down, hard. Immediately a loud siren sounded throughout the mine.

Chuttle was the first to look towards the entrance and see the guard fumbling for his gun. He snatched Mo's gun from her, aimed and fired another stun shot at the guard, hitting him directly in the chest and sending him slumped to the floor again.

"I guess that alarm is for us. We'd better get moving."

"But how are we going to escape?" asked a nervous Maffee.

"We could have used the JXX7 but there's not enough room for all three of us," Mo said looking at the huge bulk of Chuttle. "But if we could get to the communications room, we could contact the government and then all we'd have to do is avoid getting captured or shot until help arrives."

"Sounds good to me. Where's the communications room?" asked Chuttle.

"I saw a room like that when I was searching the thirty-ninth floor," said Maffee.

"Right, let's get moving then. And Maffee, try to keep up," Chuttle smiled as he spoke to Maffee, but Maffee wasn't impressed.

The three of them headed back to the lift. As they stepped inside, Chuttle stopped.

"Wait a minute," he went back to the guard's desk and looked around before bending down to pick up his laser pistol, sonic flash grenades, solid beam rapier and the gold key. "I couldn't leave without my babies."

Chuttle ran back into the lift, inserted the golden key and pressed the buttons for the thirty-fifth floor.

When the lift doors opened Chuttle stepped out, but put his arm up, indicating to Mo and Maffee not to move. He looked left and right and down the corridor straight in front of them to make sure it was clear.

"OK. Come on. Which way is the communications room Maffee."

"I'm not sure, I don't remember exactly, but it's definitely on this floor."

"Superbrain, strikes again. We'll just have to check every room. But keep moving fast because the sensors are going to be looking for us."

"I think we should start down here. I remember going this way first," Maffee pointed to the corridor straight ahead of them.

Together they checked each room as they came to it, starting with the dark cupboard that Maffee had first hidden in. Before entering each door, Chuttle would push Maffee and Mo to one side and then slowly and quietly check the room holding his laser pistol in front of him. He would peer inside to see whether or not anyone was in the room and then signal that it was all clear. As it was still night time, most of the rooms were empty, a few rooms had workers in them but none of them paid any attention to the doors as they opened and closed.

After checking about seven rooms their luck ran out. They heard the sound of many sets of boots running towards them from around the next corner.

"That doesn't sound good. We'd better switch to plan B," said Chuttle.

"What's plan B?" asked Mo.

"We run away very quickly and try to think of a plan C. Come on!"

Chapter Twenty Two

Maffee was trying his best to keep up, but was falling further behind Chuttle and Mo. He cursed his own metal legs for being so slow as he watched Chuttle dashing ahead of him. He was amazed at how swiftly the big bear could move. But that thought left him as an extreme burning sensation tore into his right arm and he was instantly thrown off his feet and flung forward.

Chuttle was looking ahead, searching for an escape route. At the same time he kept listening for the clank-clank sound of Maffee's footsteps to make sure his friend didn't get left behind. All of a sudden the clank-clank stopped and Chuttle saw Maffee fly past with black smoke pouring from his right side. Maffee's metal body crashed to the floor and tumbled over six or seven times before falling still. Maffee had been hit by one of the guards' proton bolts, projecting him forward. Without missing a step, Chuttle kept on running. Then, as he reached Maffee he bent down and scooped the metal body up with one arm. Maffee groaned. Chuttle accelerated and dodged left down a main corridor and into a group of Blista's guards running towards him.

"Stay behind me!" he ordered Mo and continued to sprint, bending forward before the guards could aim their weapons. He steam-rolled into them like a bowling ball wiping out all ten pins.

"St-rike suckers. When the Chuttle is coming, you better start running, 'cos if you get in my way, I'll roll you like hay."

"Ohhh" Maffee groaned.

"Don't worry my metal friend, I'm getting us out of here."

They kept running until Chuttle saw what he was looking for. "A lift!"

They ran towards the end of the corridor. Mo pressed the button to call the lift while Chuttle drew his gun from inside his jacket. At the other end of the corridor the guards turned the corner and Chuttle opened fire sending them scurrying back.

The lift doors opened and Chuttle ran inside with Maffee and Mo. He pressed the up button, hoping to come out near the landing deck. From there he could easily steal one of Blista's ships and make their escape. He looked down at Maffee. The smoke had stopped coming out of his side. Chuttle thought that was a good sign.

"How're you doing buddy? Are you ok? Don't worry, we're almost out of here. Once I get my hands on a ship we'll be home and dry."

"Let me have a look at him." Mo said. Chuttle stood Maffee up by holding on to his neck, while Mo looked at the damage caused by the guards.

"Hmmm, it's not too bad. He'll need a new arm and some circuits will need re-lighting, but he'll be fine. I think the shock might have caused his system to shut down temporarily."

"Well it's a good job the Chuttle doesn't know what fear is. It's danger that keeps me ticking." With that he picked Maffee up and put him under one arm, keeping his gun ready in the other.

The lift stopped and the doors began to open. A string of lasers came firing through the gap.

"Close the doors!" Mo cried out.

Chuttle pressed the button and the doors closed. Then he pressed another to stop the lift from moving.

"Why have you done that?" Mo asked.

"There's no point going down again. There'll be guards on every floor by now."

"So what are we going to do? It won't take them long to blast through the door."

Chuttle looked at Mo with a smile on his face. "I have a plan. Stand in that corner and cover your head."

"What?"

"Stand in the corner and cover your head," as he repeated the instruction he aimed his gun at the ceiling and fired three blasts. Small pieces of ceiling fell to the floor. When Mo looked up there was a wide circle missing from the ceiling.

"Hold him for me," Chuttle leaned Maffee against the far wall and Mo made sure that he didn't fall.

Chuttle then jumped and pulled himself up through the hole.

"Right, now you two," he leaned back through the hole and grabbed Maffee's head pulling him up. Then Mo reached up with both arms and Chuttle helped her through the hole. They stood on top of the lift, except for Maffee who was lying down.

"Whatever your plan is, you better do it quickly," said Mo. "That door isn't going to hold much longer."

"Don't worry. It's all under control." Chuttle looked up, studying the various light beam cables that controlled the lift's movements.

"Hmm, let's see. If I get this right then I need to cut this cable here and re-attach it here and hopefully the lift won't fall."

"Well I hope so too," said Mo.

Chuttle took out the small solid beam mini-rapier that he had taken from the Brevetar weapons dealer. He sliced through one of the green light beam cables, holding on to the top of it. He then pushed the end he was holding against the thick grey light beam cable, which instantly melted the two together, talking as he worked.

"You know, it's a good job Maffee isn't conscious. He'd be panicking so much his other arm would have probably fallen off too."

He bent down and picked up Maffee, putting him under one arm and grabbed hold of the grey cable with his other hand. "OK, you're going to have to help me here. You'll have to hold onto me and then take this gun and fire it at that red cable when I say so."

Mo wrapped one arm around Chuttle's neck and her legs around his waist then aimed the gun at the red cable.

Sparks were beginning to fly in the lift below them as the

guards' lasers and protons worked through the door. Suddenly there was a loud bang as the lift doors finally gave in to the repeated blasts. Four guards rushed into the lift with weapons drawn, looking for the three fugitives.

"Now!" Chuttle shouted at Mo.

She pulled the trigger. A flash of light lit up the lift shaft as the laser severed the red light-beam cable sending the lift hurtling down the shaft with the guards still inside it and leaving Chuttle hanging on to the grey cable with one arm.

"OK, hold tight." He used his legs to push away from the wall and swung on the cable towards the open lift door. At the last minute he let go of the cable and all three of them crashed onto the corridor floor.

Chuttle was quick to his feet and picked up Maffee. "Let's go find a ship."

Mo stood up and followed Chuttle as he ran down the corridor.

At the first set of doors they came to, Chuttle pushed the green pad, his gun ready. The doors opened to reveal a large storeroom. "Nope, that's not it."

They continued running. The next door he opened was some sort of control room, with three of Blista's guards inside. Chuttle quickly closed the door again and blasted the access panel to keep it closed. "There's got to be a ship up here somewhere."

They carried on running, trying every door they came to until they came to the end of the corridor. "Well we can go left or right, but I'm thinking right is probably the best option.

"How do you know?" asked Mo.

As she spoke lasers came shooting towards them from three guards who had just appeared at the bottom of the corridor on the left.

"Because we definitely don't want to go that way. Come on!" said Chuttle as he started running again.

They dodged around corners, checking doors as they ran, trying to find the landing bay. As they turned each corner, more guards seemed to be joining the chase behind them.

"Here. This door looks promising," Chuttle called as he ran towards a large grey door at the end of the corridor. The door opened and Chuttle and Mo ran into a stairwell.

"Oh boy, I guess we weren't at the top after all. I thought Blista said there weren't any stairs on the mine. Come on then, the only way is up!" Chuttle began leaping two steps at a time, still clinging onto Maffee under one arm. Mo followed behind him, managing to leap up the stairs at the same rate as Chuttle. She was pleased now that she had joined the local aero-gym a year ago.

"Where does this lead to?" she called up to Chuttle.

"We must be at the top of the mine by now, and at the top of the mine are the landing bays. We'll look for the fastest ship and get ourselves out of here."

"What if it's not the landing bays?"

"It must be. What else is at the top of the mines?"

They climbed three more flights of stairs, keeping close to the wall to avoid the laser shots from the guards who were close now following them up the stairwell.

Chuttle was first to reach the top of the stairs. In front of him was another large grey door. He pressed the door pad to open it but nothing happened.

"Access code required," a mechanical voice inside the door pad said.

"Access code! How's this for a code?" Chuttle drew his gun and fired a single shot at the door pad. Sparks flew, but the door remained closed.

"Now what?" asked Mo desperately. "Do something!"

Chuttle dropped Maffee to the floor and grabbed the edge of

the door with his finger tips and began to pull. He gritted his teeth and strained to pull the door open. Mo moved underneath his arms and grabbed the door too. Slowly the door slid back a little. Chuttle let out a roar as he pulled. The door started to move further back, until there was room for them all to squeeze through. Chuttle turned and fired a few shots back down the stairs towards the guards, then picked up Maffee and ran through the door after Mo.

They were now in a small grey room, no bigger than a broom cupboard. A single light-patch on the ceiling provided a dim light. The room was empty, but there was one other door leading out of it. The guards were almost at the top of the stairs now. Chuttle pressed the door pad and as the door opened he jumped through carrying Maffee and pulling Mo through with his other hand. He then quickly let go of Mo, spun around and fired one shot at the door panel. The door slid closed with a swoosh and a thud.

But they weren't in a landing bay, or a flight deck, or even another room. They were outside. Chuttle looked around and saw a desolate landscape, covered in dust and rocks with only a few, hardy bare trees. And most importantly, no air!

"Argh. I...can't...breathe. No...air..." Chuttle was choking, trying to get his breath. He dropped Maffee to the floor again and fell to his knees, clutching his throat and choking, trying desperately to grab his final breath. He rolled over onto his back and lay on the dusty ground, squirming."

Mo looked around too, but didn't seem to be panicking like Chuttle.

"Chuttle," she said calmly. "Chuttle, you can breathe. There is air here. Blista must have been lying to stop people from trying to escape!"

Chuttle looked up at her. He took his hands away from his throat and slowly breathed in. "I knew that. I was just fooling. Testing the air was ok for you guys. I wasn't panicking."

Mo gave Chuttle a sideways look then smiled. "Don't worry Chuttle. I won't tell anyone about this. The important thing is that you got us out of the mine and Blista's guards won't follow us because

144

they'll think we can't survive out here without air. But we won't have long before Blista sends them out here either with oxygen inhalers or without, depending on whether he tells them the truth about breathable air on the planet. Either way, we better get moving and try to find somewhere to hide."

Chuttle looked around at the dusty landscape stretched out before them. Whichever way he looked, North, South, East or West, the view was the same: dust, rock, stone and a few hardy but bare trees.

"I've had conversations with this canned casualty here that have been more interesting than this place. There's nothing and no way anything could survive out here. We're going to have to get back inside the mine if we want to get off this planet," he said.

"I agree. But we can't just walk back in there. We'll have to find somewhere out here to hide for a while, until it's safe to go back in."

"You're right. Let's get moving. Any preferences which way we go?" he asked.

"Not really. I can't see any flashing lights or landing strips so why don't you just lead on, before the guards pop around that door."

Chuttle picked up Maffee and began to jog with Mo. As Chuttle took deep breaths, he noticed that the air was different to the air back on Earth and many of the other planets he had visited. It seemed easier to breath and had a sweeter smell. He thought about this as they jogged along and decided it was probably because the air was cleaner and less polluted. There were no factories, cars, airships, or other buildings releasing fumes into the air.

"This air is good stuff isn't it? I feel like I could run forever. I bet you could make a fortune by bottling it up and selling it back on Earth."

"Let's just hope we get back to Earth." replied Mo solemnly.

Chapter Twenty Three

They kept running at a steady pace. The ground was soft underfoot. The scenery didn't really change much, but when Chuttle looked back over his shoulder, the entrance to the mine was just a small speck in the distance.

"We need to find some cover," he said. "I don't know how long it takes before the sun sets on this planet, but it seems to be getting darker. We don't want to get caught out when night falls. It's cold enough already."

"How about over there?" Mo said, pointing to a large mound of rocks to their right.

It was difficult to judge how far away the rocks were, but it took them another hour to reach the spot that Mo had pointed to. As they got nearer to the rocks, it was clear that what they thought was a large mound, was more like a mini mountain.

"There could be a cave in here somewhere. Let's look around," said Chuttle.

They walked a full circle around the mountain of rocks but couldn't find any gaps or crevices large enough to give them shelter, and more importantly, to hide them from any of the men that Blista was sure to send looking for them.

"You stay here with Maffee. I'll climb up and see if there's any shelter up there." Chuttle said. Then he lay Maffee down on the ground and bounded up the rocks.

Soon, Mo lost sight of him. Occasionally she heard small stones tumbling down the side of the rockface and assumed it must be Chuttle climbing around. What she didn't see were the small sets of eyes that would open from within the rocks and watch her when her back was turned.

Chuttle came bounding down again and landed by Mo's side. "Up here, there's a gap in the rocks that widens into a large enough cavern for us, it isn't five star but at least we'll be sheltered from the wind."

Chuttle led the way up the rocks. It wasn't a difficult climb but Mo was starting to feel tired. They had done a lot of running to escape the guards and now night was falling she was starting to feel the cold. Her legs felt heavy and stiff as she watched Chuttle bound effortlessly up the rocks.

"How much further do we have to climb?" she moaned.

"Not far now, just around this corner."

Chuttle leapt around the side of the rocks and Mo lost sight of him until she too turned the corner and saw him waiting for her, holding Maffee under one arm. "Are we there yet?" she said, with her hands on her hips, breathing heavily.

"Yep."

"Well where's the cave?"

"It's here." Chuttle shifted to one side and nodded towards a small, dark opening by his legs.

"In there? Can you fit through there?" Mo asked.

"It's a squeeze but I can make it. Once you get through the gap, it looks like it opens out into quite a large passageway."

Chuttle bent down on all fours and pushed Maffee through the gap.

"Do you want me to go first so that I can pull you through, in case you get stuck?" Mo asked.

Chuttle looked at her crossly. "I'm not going to get stuck. I've been in tighter spots than this. Just relax and follow me."

His head fitted through the gap quite easily but there was no way his shoulders would get through squarely. Mo watched as he twisted and turned forcing one shoulder and arm through and then the other. Next he shuffled in order to squeeze his torso through a couple of inches at a time. Then he stopped. Mo had to stop herself from laughing as she realised his bottom was firmly wedged in the gap.

"Hurry up, it's getting cold out here," she teased.

More strange noises came from Chuttle as he tried to get through. "You're going to have to give me a push, I think I'm stuck, it must be these loose fitting trousers."

"OK, here goes," Mo bent down, placing one hand on each of Chuttle's cheeks and pushed as hard as she could, but Chuttle's rear stayed wedged exactly where it was. She pushed again but with no effect. She stood up.

"Let's try one cheek at a time," she said as she took up position behind Chuttle's left side. She dug her feet into the ground and pushed as hard as she could.

"That's it, keep pushing," called Chuttle. "Now try the other side."

Mo changed position to concentrate on Chuttle's right side. Slowly the right side moved through the gap until suddenly Chuttle popped forward, leaving only his legs sticking out of the gap at Mo's side. He pulled himself through and called out to Mo.

"Your turn."

As Mo slid through the gap she joked with Chuttle. "Don't be embarrassed Chuttle, you can't help being big."

But Chuttle wasn't embarrassed at all, he had an answer for everything.

"That's right. I can't help it if the muscles on my behind are so big. My physique is a gift."

Mo stood up. Chuttle was right, as soon as they had crawled through the entrance, the cavern opened up allowing her to stand up straight, although Chuttle had to stoop over a little, so as not to bang his head on the ceiling. Chuttle took out the mini solid beam rapier. Its blade lit up providing a dim glow that allowed them to see a few paces in front and around them.

The walls were dark in the cave, unlike the walls of the mine which had been glistening the reddish brown colour of rusdan. The

148

ground was also different. It seemed harder, more solid underfoot. Outside of the cave their footsteps had been cushioned by the amount of dust and sand on the ground, but inside the cave the ground was strangely, spotlessly clean. Chuttle decided that it wasn't worth wasting time thinking about the ground and started walking.

"Come on. Let's find somewhere to rest for the night. The floor's not going to be very comfortable for you to sleep on. I'll bet by the end of the night you'll wish you had my extra padding," Chuttle grinned and patted his own large rear end.

Mo followed Chuttle through the cave, staying close behind to benefit from the glow of his knife. Occasionally she would turn around to try and see behind them, but it was too dark. She couldn't help feeling that they were being watched.

"Do you think anything lives on this planet, apart from in the mine?" she asked.

"Are you kidding! The place is a desert. Nothing could live out here. I sure wouldn't. Anything that tried to live out here for too long would find themselves starving, dieing of thirst, without shelter and worst of all, probably bored to death. There's absolutely no reason for being on this planet, unless you're one of Blista's mob. It's the dullest planet I've ever seen, just a few rocks, some trees that dried up years ago and a lot of sand."

"Well it feels like we're being watched all the time, but maybe that's because I've been locked up in Blista's cell for so long surrounded by cameras all night and day," Mo said as she looked around again.

"I'd say this is the last place anyone will be watching you. Be careful here, the path starts to lead downhill and there are a few steps."

They continued to walk downwards, deeper into the mountain. After a while Mo was too tired to think about being watched. Her eyes focused on the path ahead, making sure she didn't trip or lose her footing. But the path was quite smooth. There weren't any loose stones or jagged rocks along the way. Just a few well placed steps that seemed to be conveniently placed to help them descend further down into the mountain.

"It's almost as if this place was built this way. But who'd build a tunnel, inside a bunch of rocks, in the middle of a deserted planet, that no-one knows about?" Chuttle was thinking to himself but talking out loud.

"Hmm," said Mo, too tired to pay attention. She carried on following Chuttle downwards until he stopped.

"This is it. Not the most comfortable place, but at least we're out of the night air and hidden from Blista's men."

Mo looked up and saw that they were in a large cavern, about the size of her office back home, but with a ceiling twice as high.

"We should try to get some rest. Tomorrow we have to find a way back into the mine and then off this planet. This spot looks as good as any." Chuttle put Maffee down on the ground, then sat down against the wall of the cavern. Mo flopped down next to him.

"You know. We've walked so far down inside this mountain thing, I'd say we're probably back down to ground level. I think that's why the ground is so dusty here but clean everywhere else."

"Hmm," was all Mo could say again. Her eyes were already shut and she drifted off to sleep with her head resting on Chuttle's arm.

Chuttle looked down at Mo then said to himself. "Well Chuttle, you're finally doing it. The safety of the whole Universe lies in your hands. This is what you've been waiting for all your life. You finally get to prove you're a hero. No time for fear, hesitation or mistakes. When tomorrow comes you've got to think smart and act fast. What happens next will shape the rest of your life. You'll be remembered as Chuttle, the greatest Space Detective to ever cross the skies. It's Chuttle-time, my time," he said proudly.

"Chuttle, go to sleep," Mo said sleepily.

Chapter Twenty Four

Chuttle and Mo's eyes sprang open at the same time as the ground began to rumble and shake. Rocks began to tumble down all around them. Chuttle pulled Mo's head to his chest and tried to cover both of them with his arms. He braced himself expecting at any second to be hit by the falling rocks, but amazingly all of the rocks seemed to fall clear of them until eventually they stopped falling altogether. Chuttle moved his arms cautiously and looked up. The cavern they had been in was gone, above him all he could see was the dark night sky and bright stars, there were no high rock walls and no ceiling. Instead, all the rocks that had been tumbling down were now spread out in a circle all around Chuttle and Mo. Mo looked too and then had to blink and look again. The rocks were staring back at them! Each of the rocks, no matter what its size, had a small grey eye shining from the rest of its dark body.

"What's going on Chuttle? What are they?" Mo asked, not taking her eyes from the rocks.

"Unbelievable. I've heard of these things but I've never seen one. I wasn't even sure if they really existed. They're Grocktars, living rock-like creatures that think, move and live, usually on deserted planets where there is no other race or species."

"Are they dangerous?" Mo asked nervously.

"Nothing is too dangerous for Chuttle, but let's not waste time waiting to find out. Follow me, it's time to break our way out."

"Hold on a minute. If these things were going to hurt us they could have crushed us while we were sleeping. They might be able to help us."

"Are you crazy? Look at them. Even if they're not with Blista, how could they help us, they're bits of rock with an eye. They probably can't understand what we're saying, that's if they can hear what we're saying because they haven't even got ears. I doubt that we'd be able to explain who we are, why we're here and what we need. And somehow, I doubt that these guys have got a spacecraft that we could use to get out of here. So like I said, there's no point wasting time, let's just get out of here."

151

Without waiting for Mo to argue, Chuttle picked up Maffee and ran towards the rocks. He lowered his shoulder and charged as hard as he could into one of the largest Grocktars that was almost as big as he was. There was a thud as Chuttle hit it, but the rock stayed firmly in place. Chuttle held his shoulder and turned back to Mo with a look of pain on his face. "Ow. These things are pretty tough."

"They're rocks Chuttle. And rocks tend to be pretty tough."

Chuttle continued to rub his shoulder. "Maybe we should try to communicate with them instead."

He turned around to face the Grocktar that he had just run into and with a big smile on his face said, "Hi."

The large Grocktar slowly began to roll forward. It pushed against Chuttle and kept on pushing. "Oh you want to play do you? Come on then." Chuttle put his hands on the rock and growled as he started pushing against it. But the rock was too strong. Digging his feet into the ground Chuttle used all his might to push against the rock, but it kept rolling forward, pushing Chuttle closer and closer towards the other Grocktars behind him until he felt his back against another large Grocktar.

"Ok, you win rock-man," said Chuttle and he gave up. But the Grocktar kept on pushing and Chuttle found himself being squeezed tighter and tighter between the two rocks, unable to move. The pressure against his chest was making it difficult for him to breath. Desperately he reached out with one arm and grabbed a small fist-sized Grocktar that had perched on top of a larger rock in order to get a better view. With his other hand he pulled his gun from his side and pointed it at the small Grocktar. Immediately the large Grocktar loosened his grip on Chuttle, without letting him go.

"Back off now or the little guy gets it," said Chuttle, now able to breathe again.

"No Chuttle!" It was Mo who shouted at Chuttle. "You can't hurt it. It must be just a baby."

"It's just a rock."

"It doesn't matter. It's still a baby. Now put it down."

"Look, I'm not really going to hurt it, I'm just trying to get us out of here." He explained to Mo.

The small rock was watching Chuttle with its eye. Chuttle could feel it trembling in his hand. "Oh alright." He slowly put the rock back down and braced himself to be squashed again, but instead of being squeezed, the two large Grocktars loosened their hold on him. Chuttle and Mo watched as the rocks behind Chuttle fanned out to form a U shape around him. The big Grocktar then gave him a slight nudge backwards. Chuttle took a step back and all the other rocks rolled forward slightly. The big rock nudged him again.

"They must want us to go with them somewhere," said Mo.

"Well we've got as much choice as a man travelling down a one way street with no brakes, no steering and a herd of Sharag Wildebeest pushing from the rear." Chuttle picked up Maffee and started walking.

"What if they're taking us back to Blista?" Asked Mo when she caught up with Chuttle.

"Then that little fella will be the first one I blow to pieces, followed quickly by as many more as it takes to get away again. But I don't think these Grocktars are working for Blista."

"How do you know?"

"It's just a Space Detective's hunch. And when you're in the crime fighting business you learn when to trust a hunch."

"So where are they taking us?"

"Hm. I don't know. Maybe to meet the Rock Ruler, or the Grocktar Governor, or the Senior Stone! I guess we just go with the flow and see where we come out."

They kept walking, guided by the Grocktars that surrounded them. Mo was fascinated by the way the Grocktars moved. They rolled as if they were on a gentle slope, even when they came to rough ground they would roll effortlessly up and down as though running on a powerful engine. As their grey granite turned, the single eye stayed exactly where it was, the same height, facing the same direction. The eye looked as if it was just floating unconnected over the surface of the Grocktar.

After a while Mo realised that she had lost track of time. She couldn't tell how long they had been walking. Blista's men had taken all of her possessions, even her watch when they had first kidnapped her. "How long have we been walking?" she asked Chuttle.

"About three hours. If we were going back to the mine we'd have been able to see it by now. The only thing I can see apart from desert and more desert is that mountain in the distance and it looks like that's where we're heading, although who knows if it's really a mountain or friends and relatives of these lot," he nodded towards the Grocktars.

They continued to walk without talking. Mo was thinking about her home, her parents and being back on Earth. Chuttle was thinking about how he could escape, trying to put a plan together to get back to the mine, find a spacecraft and avoid the planet's missile systems that had almost shot his Dragonfly when they first tried to land on Suvmar.

Chapter Twenty Five

Finally the Grocktars stopped rolling and Chuttle and Mo could stop walking. Day was beginning to break and the sun was rising. In front of them was a huge tower of dark rock, lifeless and still.

Chuttle looked around at the Grocktars, "So what now guys, do we climb over, go around or are the walls going to part and let us walk through?"

Mo jumped as hundreds of eyes popped open on the wall in front of them. There was a rumbling as two enormous Grocktars from the wall moved aside leaving a large doorway. "I guess we go this way," said Chuttle and walked through the doorway still carrying Maffee under his arm.

Chuttle and Mo both stopped in amazement as they passed through the wall. It was like walking into a different world. In front of them was a beautiful garden full of flowers, trees and grass. There were different fruit, vegetable and grain growing in small, neatly planted patches, each adding a different colour to the spectrum of the garden. Mo couldn't believe that such a beautiful place could exist on such a lifeless planet. There were even a few thin trees, and as she looked up she saw that each one was thick with rich, green leaves. She continued to look upwards expecting to see the sun, blazing down through bright blue skies, but instead of the sky she saw a ceiling of more dark rocks and attached to them somehow were thousands of small lights, giving out a glow that resembled almost perfect sunlight.

"Wow," said Mo.

"Make mine a double wow," said Chuttle.

Even the sound of the two large Grocktars closing the doorway behind them didn't distract Chuttle and Mo from the amazing view.

"Hello there!" Chuttle and Mo were surprised by the sound of another person's voice. Chuttle quickly drew his gun from his side and looked around to spot the owner of the voice. An elderly dark, tall man walked towards them. He had curly grey hair and was wearing an untied robe that trailed along the floor behind him. Underneath the robe he wore a pair of khaki shorts and a shirt with the top three buttons undone.

"Hello," the man repeated as he drew nearer. "How wonderful it is to see you. Wonderful." The man either ignored or did not see the gun that Chuttle was pointing at him. Instead he put out his hand. Mo stepped forward and shook it.

"I am King Mukuto Rawali Savmarta the fourth, but people call me King Mukuto. I am very honoured to meet you." He lifted Mo's hand and gently kissed it. King Mukuto spoke slowly, clearly pronouncing every word.

"I'm Mo Draper and this is Chuttle."

Mukuto released Mo's hand and extended his arm towards Chuttle. "You won't need your gun here Mr Chuttle, I have no reason to treat you as an enemy."

Chuttle thought about this briefly then said, "Well yours is the friendliest face I've seen since I arrived on this planet so I guess I can trust you. I'm Chuttle, the Universal number one Space Detective, I'm a crime fighter, a wrong righter, I shake down crime and take out the grime, where evil is hiding, I come in riding. Where the bad dudes are staying, I come in blazin'..."

King Mukuto held up his hand to interrupt Chuttle. "Please, I think I understand what you mean but let us not stand here talking. You must be tired and hungry from your long walk. Please come to my home, I have prepared refreshments and you can rest. Then perhaps we will be able to do something to help your friend," he said looking at Maffee.

"I could certainly manage a snack or two. I'm as hungry as a wolf, and you know what they say, a hungry wolf has a feint heart. Not that I'm faint hearted, but I am hungry." Chuttle said, rubbing his empty stomach.

King Mukuto turned and led them through the gardens until they came to a small home built into the rocks.

Inside the house, Chuttle's eyes immediately fell onto a long table covered in dishes of food. "Help yourselves," said the King.

Chuttle lay Maffee down on a chair and started to eat from the range of food on the table. There was nothing he didn't like. It all tasted fresh and delicious. Mo ate too. There was plenty to choose from, fruits, breads, beans, pulses and vegetables, all flavoured with varieties of spices and herbs.

Eventually they both had eaten enough to make up for the last few hours that they had had to endure without food and they sunk back into some soft chairs.

"So tell us King Mukuto, what are you doing on this planet and how do you survive?" asked Mo.

"Ah, that is a long story."

"Well I'm not moving from this spot for a good while yet, so fire away," said Chuttle.

"Well, for many years this planet was a beautiful, green paradise. There were thousands of us living here in peace. There was no fighting, no war and no crime. As a race of people, we kept ourselves to ourselves, with little need to deal with other planets. We were self sufficient, we grew all the food we needed. Our industry and technology were probably very basic compared to larger planets, but we had enough for our needs.

"You should have seen Suvmar back then. It was so full of life and fun. People were happy with their lives, the land was rich with the colour of flowers, fruits and trees. Rivers flowed with clear, fresh water and animals and birds roamed freely. It was a perfect world."

King Mukuto's face lit up as he recalled the former glory of his planet, picturing in his mind the way it had once been.

"But then, one day Gelt Blista came to see me. He said he had a business proposition that would make Suvmar rich and important, bringing visitors from all over the Universe. He wanted to set up a Rusdan mine.

"I told him no, we did not need or want any mining facility on

Suvmar and we did not want visitors from all over the galaxy, bringing with them their greed and crime and corruption. He came back to Suvmar two or three times trying to persuade me to let him build his mine here, but each time I refused."

"Why refuse man. Sounds like Blista could have made you all rich?" said Chuttle from the seat he had chosen to recline in.

"I refused because I couldn't let him dig, drill and destroy our planet. But most importantly I couldn't let him harm our friends, the Grocktars. You have seen how the Grocktars are a living part of this planet. But Blista sees them just as rocks that are in his way. Men like him have no regard for others and no respect for their environment. So he left. But he's not one to take no for an answer. He said we were making a mistake that we would all regret!"

King Mukuto paused, his eyes looking downwards, remembering terrible events. He continued to talk, but he was quieter now, almost whispering.

"They must have come during the night. Some of my people said they had seen ships flying low across the land, but we did not know then what they were doing. It was only when people and animals began to fall sick that I realised. Blista's men had poisoned our water, all of it, seas, rivers and lakes. He had used fast breeding poison or some sort of virus that spread so quickly that we couldn't reverse it. Soon there was no fresh water to drink, or to water our land. Many people and animals grew sick and died before we realised the reason, but worse was to come. Sea and river levels began to fall. Each day you could see the difference. Our planet was drying up before our eyes and there was nothing we could do. Whatever poison Blista had used was somehow also evaporating all the water and moisture from our planet.

"Eventually I had to make the decision and order everyone to leave Suvmar. My people took all they could carry and left in their spacecrafts."

"Where did they go?" asked Mo.

"Nearby planets. Some of the younger ones were more adventurous and took the opportunity to go further into space, but the

158

result was the same. In the end I was the only one left on Suvmar. Left to watch the last animals slowly die out, then watch the crops and trees wither and fall and eventually see the land itself turned into a parched, barren waste."

"Why didn't you leave too?"

"I am the king of Suvmar. My father was king before me and his father before him and all our fathers' fathers to the beginning of the planet. I could not leave. Instead I decided to stay here and wait for the day that Blista and his mine are stopped. Then I will go out, find my people and bring them back and we will bring life to Suvmar again."

"So when's that going to be?" asked Chuttle.

King Mukuto looked at Chuttle and said, "That depends on you, doesn't it Chuttle?" He smiled a slight smile.

"Me. How does it depend on me?"

"You are Chuttle. It's your dream is it not, to save the Universe? The Universe is a big place, to save it you have to start somewhere, what makes you think your destiny does not begin here, with the fate of Suvmar?"

For once, Chuttle had nothing to say. Instead he stayed quiet, thinking about what King Mukuto had said. It was Mo who broke the silence. "You must have been lonely all this time without company or anyone to talk to."

"I have company. I talk with the Grocktars. They may not be very active, but we can communicate."

"They can talk?" Mo said, amazed.

"Of course, but not as you and I are talking. You cannot hear what they say out loud, only in your head, it is like a language of thought that can be directed to another person's brain. But it is a special skill that is not easy for everyone to learn. How do you think I knew you were coming?"

"But how can you live here without water? How have you got

159

these beautiful gardens?"

"Water capsules. There were many stored on the planet before everyone left, and with the recycling plant I am able to create a small amount of water, enough to maintain the gardens that you see. And as you have seen, the artificial sunlight helps the plants to grow."

"Amazing," was all that Mo could say.

It was Chuttle who spoke next. He had been thinking about what the King had said and it had re-ignited his heroic ambitions. "So, when everyone left, did they take all of the spacecrafts or did they leave some behind?"

"Oh no, some were left behind. Many people shared the journey in larger ships, so a few ships weren't used. But over the years they have been neglected. The weather has destroyed them and all that's left is decaying metal that's mostly buried by drifting sand and dust."

"Typical! That's just our luck, nothing is ever easy," said Chuttle.

"Except for one ship that is."

Chuttle looked up at King Mukuto.

"My ship is sheltered here within the compound. As I say, one day I will use it to go out and find my people and lead them back to Suvmar."

"Yes! We can use it to get off this planet and get back to Earth. Then Miss Draper can tell the InterEarth government about Blista, get him locked up, shut down the mine and you'll have your planet back. Where's the ship?"

"It is protected by Grocktars. I will take you to it. It is not very modern I am afraid, it is all manual controls but I can run through them with you. You will pick it up easily."

"No problem. If it's got wings, I can fly it," Chuttle said confidently.

160

Mo pushed herself out of her comfortable seat and walked over to where Maffee was lying. "While you two are gone I'll stay here and see if I can get Maffee back on his feet."

"If we can get the ship flying, I reckon we'll be ready to go pretty soon, so see if you can get him patched up and ready to roll by then," said Chuttle.

King Mukuto fetched Mo a tool kit from another room and then led Chuttle out of the house. They walked a short distance to another mound of rocks, which Chuttle guessed were Grocktars. As they got nearer, four large Grocktars at the front of the mound moved aside revealing the nose cone of an old-fashioned but very well maintained shining chrome space craft. He could tell it was old fashioned by the liquid rocket boosters at the back of the ship. All modern ships used Rusdan energy for power instead of liquid rockets. But although it was old, it was in perfect condition.

"Oh boy, you're full of surprises. She's older than my mother, but a classic, a real classic. It's a 22-50 Ahdon Cruiser isn't it?" Chuttle said as he took a closer look at the ship.

"Correct. I bought it brand new. It was state of the art back then. She has only flown once, I hope everything still works."

"It's bound to. In those days things were built to last. More reliable than an old dog. I've always wanted to fly one of these beauties. To feel the rumbling of all that raw, rocket fuelled power pushing you forward. Using the stick to take her wherever you want to go. Is she carrying weapons?"

"Oh no. As I said, we are a peaceful people. I had no reason to want weapons. Do you think you will need them?"

"Who knows? But when you're in my business, it's always best to have them just in case."

As Chuttle stepped closer to the cruiser its lights switched on automatically. A door just behind the nose cone silently slid open and a set of steps hissed down towards the ground. Chuttle couldn't wait to see inside the cruiser and bounded up the stairs. "Come on King, let's get this beauty moving and groovin'!"

Chapter Twenty Six

Bang! Bang! Crash!

Explosions rocked the ground. Chuttle and King Mukuto ran out of the shelter covering the cruiser then dashed back inside as Grocktars of all sizes fell towards them from above.

"Is that supposed to happen?" asked Chuttle. But King Mukuto had a shocked look on his face that suggested to Chuttle that it wasn't.

From just inside the shelter, Chuttle looked up to see the Grocktars that had formed the roof of the cavern falling to the ground and clear blue sky above. Two black fighter craft came into view followed closely by a much larger troop carrier.

Mo stepped out of the doorway of King Mukuto's house. Behind her came Maffee without his right arm. "What's going on?" Mo shouted across to Chuttle.

"Blista must have found us," he shouted back, then turning to the King he said "How *did* he find us?"

"I do not know," said the King, his world falling apart around him.

The three black space craft descended through the hole that they had blasted in the roof. It looked like they were getting ready to land.

"Come on King. We're getting out of here. It's time to test your cruiser." Chuttle ran back up the stairs and into the cruiser.

The three black craft landed without a care, crushing crops and flowers. Doors on the carrier quickly opened and about forty of Blista's guards leapt out with their guns ready. Mo and Maffee stood where they were. King Mukuto stepped forward.

"I am King Mukuto Rawali Savmarta the Fourth. You are on my planet and I demand to know why."

The guards didn't answer. They stood still with their guns pointed at the King.

"Well? I am waiting for an answer. Which of you is in charge?"

The door of one of the fighter craft slowly opened. Detective Lychee marched down the steps and stood between the guards.

"I'm in charge. I'm Detective Lychee and I've come for him, her and the big furry one." Lychee pointed at Maffee, Mo and then looked around for Chuttle.

"Detective Lychee!" Maffee exclaimed. "It's alright now, we've found Miss Draper. She'll tell you that it wasn't us that kidnapped her, it was Blista and his guards. We were only trying to help."

"Don't worry Maffee. I know all about it. I know you are innocent and I know that it was Gelt Blista who took Miss Draper. But the great thing about all this is that no-one else will ever know because you three will be working in a Rusdan mine for the rest of your lives while my boss, that's Mr Blista, takes over Earth and then does whatever he wants."

"The cheek of it!" said Maffee, "You're supposed to be a trooper. It's disgraceful, despicable."

"Save your fancy talk metal-head, we're taking you all back to the mine."

"Not so fast Detective." King Mukuto took a step forward. "What if we don't want to come with you?"

"You don't have much choice. You see there's only three of you, or four including the Pervian bear, although he seems to have already deserted you. So there's three of you and forty of us, which basically means that you do whatever I say."

"Maybe."

Suddenly a medium sized Grocktar shot forward and hurled itself into the stomach of one of Blista's guards sending him flying through the air, before crashing to the ground in a heap, winded and gasping for breath. Detective Lychee and the other guards watched,

163

not sure what had just happened. Without warning another Grocktar whirled from nowhere and crashed into the back of another guard, throwing him to the floor.

"You seem to have miscounted Detective. I think you will find there are a few more than three of us."

The Grocktars rolled forward with eyes glaring, surrounding the guards.

Detective Lychee was shocked. He'd never seen a Grocktar before, but he quickly recovered. "Don't just stand there," he shouted to his men, "Blast them all!"

All of a sudden, laser and sonic weapons began firing as Grocktars rushed towards the guards. Beams of light and pieces of rock flew in all directions.

During the commotion the Ahdon Cruiser slowly hovered out of the Grocktar shelter. "King, Maffee, Miss Draper, quick, get in!" Chuttle shouted through the cruiser's loudspeaker. Maffee and Mo began to run towards it, bending low, trying to avoid stray shots from guards' guns.

They were halfway to the cruiser when they were stopped by Detective Lychee standing in front of them with his gun in his hand. "Not so fast! You're coming with me. Move it!" There was a clank as he prodded Maffee with his gun and pointed towards one of the black fighter craft.

"I don't think so," said Mo as she watched two large Grocktars rush from both sides and squash Detective Lychee between them. There was a look of pain on his face as he slumped to the floor. Before they had time to look up again, one of the two Grocktars shattered into tiny pieces, blasted by a guard. The other Grocktar turned its eye and rocketed straight at the guard.

"Come on Maffee. Let's get to the ship," Mo said, pushing Maffee forward.

As they ran another guard stepped in front of them. Without pausing, Mo struck the guard with the toolkit she was carrying, knocking him to the ground. But as she tried to run he grabbed her ankle. "Keep running. I'll catch up with you," she shouted to Maffee and then turned around and started to kick the guard's hand with her other foot.

Maffee watched Mo trying to release the guard's grip from her ankle. As he did so he saw a bright flash from behind her. She looked up in shock and then in pain. She had been shot. Maffee watched, stunned. Everything seemed to be happening in slow motion. He had never seen anyone killed before, he had never experienced the death of anyone he knew. The shouting voices around him just became noise, he lost sight of everything else except for Mo's body falling lifeless to the ground. It was getting further away from him. He wasn't aware of Chuttle grabbing him and dragging him back to the cruiser. He could only focus on Mo. She disappeared as the ship's door closed. Chuttle dropped Maffee into his seat and started the cruisers engines.

"You think you can take her from us? I'll show you. You're messing with the wrong dude. You're messing with Chuttle, the Universe's number one space detective, and you're gonna wish you had never heard that name!"

He pulled back on the sticks and the ship lifted about ten feet off the ground. He slowly hovered until he was over the spot where Mo was lying. There was a wide circle of Blista's guards around her body now. "Try this for size Chumps!" Chuttle flicked a switch and there was a roar of engines as the exhausts sprang to life like a smoke breathing dragon. A powerful jet of smoke and fumes shot from the back of the cruiser blasting Blista's men who stood in its way. Chuttle slowly began to turn the ship on the spot until the whole circle of guards were lying on their backs some twenty yards away from where they had been standing. He quickly lowered the cruiser, got out of his seat, and picked up Mo, carrying her into the ship.

Inside the cruiser Chuttle gently placed Mo's slumped body into the seat next to Maffee then went back to the pilot's seat.

"Let's get out of here," he said taking the control sticks. With a roar of engines the cruiser rushed upwards into the sky through the hole that had been blasted by Blista's men. "Will the Grocktars be able to hold Blista's men back, King?"

"Yes, you won't have to worry about them. The Grocktars will stop them going anywhere, by the time they have finished there won't be a guard left standing."

Maffee spoke quietly from his seat, "Is she dead?" He asked looking at Mo's lifeless body.

"I'm afraid so my friend. I'm sorry I couldn't save her," Chuttle said sadly.

King Mukuto moved across the cruiser to Mo. "Well let's have a look shall we, perhaps there's something I can do. Our people are very good healers. We didn't make wars, but we were very good at healing our sick."

King Mukuto pressed the palms of his hands together as if in prayer and then pointed his fingers towards Mo's body. He closed his eyes and began to whisper so quietly that all Maffee could hear was the breath from his mouth. As Maffee watched it seemed to him as if the air between the King's fingers and Mo's body was moving, shimmering. But Mo remained still, her face pale.

King Mukuto let out a long deep breath and without opening his eyes moved his hands above Mo's heart. He began to whisper again. This time Maffee was sure the air around the King's hands was moving. He watched it closely, so closely that he didn't see Mo's eyes flutter. Then she took a sharp breath and opened her eyes. Maffee shrieked. Chuttle turned to see what was happening. "Hot smoking Joseph! How the hairy blazes are you alive?"

"What happened?" asked Mo.

"You were shot. Zapped by a proton light charge. You were dead and now you're not," said Chuttle.

"Well I feel fine. Not dead at all. What happened to the guards?"

"The Grocktars have taken care of them. And with all the guards out there, we can go to the mine and take care of Blista!" said the King.

166

"I'm all for that," said Chuttle. "Let's go!" He turned the cruiser around and headed at full speed for the mine.

Chapter Twenty Seven

From the air it was easy for Chuttle to locate the entrance to the landing dock. He steered the cruiser to the bay next to Blista's ship.

As they stepped off the cruiser they could still hear the noises of the mine work going on, but there was no sign of any guards. Chuttle guessed that all the guards had left the mine with Detective Lychee except perhaps for a few watching over the mine workers.

"Blista could be anywhere on the mine. Where are we going to start looking?" asked Chuttle.

"Why don't we start at the JXX7?" suggested Mo.

"Good idea," replied Chuttle and he set off marching to the nearest lift with the others following him.

Chuttle, Maffee, Mo and King Mukuto entered the science lab. Chuttle had found that the laser from his pistol was just as effective at opening the voice recognition doorways. Through the glass partition they saw Blista talking to Saffa with an angry look on his face.

"It had better be ready Saffa. I need this prototype working so that we can copy it and build my fleet," shouted Blista who hadn't noticed the others in the lab.

"I assure you Mr Blista, I personally made sure that the Draper woman completed the construction."

"How do you know whether she completed it or not, she managed to knock you out and escape."

"But I'm certain she finished the JXX7 before then. We were just about to start testing it."

Blista's face became even angrier. "So it hasn't even been tested! In that case I'm telling you now Saffa, it's you who is going to be the first one to sit in that pilot's seat and try it out. So you better pray it is all working."

Saffa tried not to show that he was nervous. He wasn't keen on testing the JXX7. He wasn't certain that it was ready, but he hoped it was.

Suddenly, sensing that he was being watched, Blista turned to the entrance of the lab and saw Chuttle, Maffee, Mo and the King.

"What are you doing here? Where's Lychee?" Blista demanded.

"You could say that Lychee and his men ran into a bit of a brick wall," said Chuttle with a smile on his face.

"Unbelievable, I send Lychee with all my guards to capture a woman, a one armed robot and an oversized stuffed cushion and he can't even do that. So how did you all get here?"

"In the comfort of the Royal Cruiser, belonging to our friend King Mukuto."

"You as well! I knew it was a mistake leaving you out there in the desert. I should have had you thrown off the planet years ago when you first got in my way, but I thought no, I'll be charitable and let you stay here with your little flowers and your little trees. Well that teaches me to be so nice. Oh well, you're all here now so I suppose you've saved me the trouble of having to send more guards out to fetch you. You three can be sent back to the prison cells while you, Miss Draper, can make sure this JXX7 is ready to go. And no more funny business."

"This guy's crazier than I thought," said Chuttle. "The only place we're going is back to Earth and it's you who is going to be sitting in the prison cell from now on. In case you've forgotten, all of your guards are out in the desert, so unless this bespectacled shrimp here is a one man army," Chuttle said pointing at Saffa, "You're in no position to give anymore orders."

"Well that's where you're wrong my furry friend. You see my regular guards may be temporarily sat in the desert, but I think you'll have a harder time escaping from Blista Enterprises Armed Super Troopers, or BEASTS as I like to call them."

With a smile on his face Blista took a small communications device from his pocket and pressed a red button. Chuttle, Maffee, Mo and the King looked around expecting to hear a loud alarm, or see flashing lights, but nothing happened.

"I think you need some new batteries in that thing," said Chuttle.

"I think not," and as Blista spoke, the ceiling of the science lab crashed inwards and down dropped a dozen machines with large, dome-shaped black heads, shining metal bodies, short legs and long arms. Chuttle was the first to react, he spun around and reversed kicked one of the machines, sending it flying through the air and crashing against the far wall.

"You three step back, I'll deal with this," Chuttle ordered as he stepped forward grabbing the next robot by the back of its head and pulling it around so quickly that it didn't have time to react before it crunched into another machine, causing both to spark furiously.

As Chuttle watched the two machines fall to the floor, the long arms of another machine grabbed hold of him from behind and wrapped itself tightly around his arms and body.

"Arghh! Get off me!" Chuttle pushed himself backwards, gaining more and more speed and carrying the robot with him. The pair of them crashed hard into the wall, but the robot held on. Mo saw another machine start to move towards Chuttle with its arms raised above its head ready to strike. She moved swiftly across to Chuttle. As she got nearer, she dived across in front of him and pulled his gun out of his side pocket. She landed with a roll, raised the weapon and shot the robot that was moving towards Chuttle. She then turned to fire at the machine holding Chuttle but his huge body was blocking her shot.

"Now!" called Chuttle, and he spun around, lifting the robot off its feet so that its back was facing Mo. She fired one shot. There was a flash of light as the laser hit the metal body of the machine and it fell to the floor.

Another robot came at Chuttle, he side-stepped it and then hammered home a large fist into the side of the machine. The machine was pushed sideways by the blow, but it was Chuttle who cried out, "Owww, those things are hard," he blew on his fist trying to ease the sting. The robot recovered and started to move towards Chuttle again.

170

This time Chuttle used his foot to sweep the robot's legs away from under it. Then before it had time to stand up again Chuttle picked up a large desk and slammed it down on top of the robot.

A couple more bright flashes lit up the room as Mo took care of another two Beasts.

"Help!" Maffee's high pitched scream attracted the attention of Chuttle. He was pinned against the wall by another of the robots. It held him with one hand wrapped around his thin neck. The robot's other arm was raised and moving slowly towards Maffee's head. At the end of its arm, instead of a hand there was a whirling device that looked like an egg whisk but with much sharper blades.

"Help!" Maffee shrieked again as his weak arms tried to hold back the arm of the Beast. This time it was King Mukuto who moved first. He leapt up onto the Beast's back then pushed himself upwards so that he was standing on its head. The Beast didn't seem to notice and continued to push its blades towards Maffee. The King reached up to the ceiling light and pulled off the cover, exposing the light-beam power cables. He took a firm grip on the exposed cable and jumped off the Beast's head, pulling the cable down with him. As he landed on the floor behind the robot still holding the live light beam cable, he thrust it into the joint between the robot's body and legs. There were sparks as the robot's body went into spasms before seizing completely with its hand still wrapped around Maffee's neck. Chuttle rushed forward, jumped into the air and crashed his flying kick into the side of the frozen robot, releasing its grip on Maffee and toppling it to the floor.

As Chuttle landed he turned to face the one Beast that was still standing across the room, looking it in the eye. The robot looked back. It moved its arm slowly down to its side. A panel swished open revealing a laser pistol. The Beast's hand hovered just above the pistol, waiting. Chuttle turned to face the Beast square on. His hand moved slowly to his side, ready to draw his own gun. It was like a scene from an old-fashioned gunfight.

"Do you know who I am? I'm Chuttle, the number one Space Detective. I blow away dirtballs like you as easily as a kid blows out the candles on a birthday cake. If you mess with me, you're buying a one way ticket to Smokesville, cos I'm quicker and slicker than a dancing boy's ticker."

Mo watched as Chuttle's fingers moved slowly above his gun holster. To her horror she realised that there was no gun. She had removed it seconds before to shoot the other Beasts.

"Chuttle wait!" she cried.

"Relax. I'm taking care of business, it's all under control," Chuttle said without taking his eyes off the Beast.

"You don't understand…"

"Shh, shh, shh," Chuttle looked at Mo and winked, then turned back to look the Beast straight in the eye. "What are you waiting for you copper plated nugget. Let's get this show rolling."

With lightning speed the robot's hand pulled out its laser pistol and raised it, aiming directly at Chuttle's head, but no shot came out. Mo had been watching Chuttle's right hand, expecting him to reach for his pistol and find that it wasn't in the holster, but his right hand didn't move. She missed his left arm flick forwards to throw the solid beam mini-rapier towards the Beast. Before she had time to look up, the rapier's beam flew into the robot's body, piercing its shell and burning a hole in the Central Intelligence Bit as it passed through the body and out the other side. The lifeless robot tipped forwards and fell still on the floor.

"OK Blista, now it's your turn," said Chuttle looking across to where Saffa and Blista had been talking, but it was only Saffa who was still stood there.

"Where's he gone?"

The JXX7 lit up as Blista started the engines.

"Well Saffa, what are you waiting for man. Get in here now. We're leaving these fools." Blista called down to Saffa.

Saffa looked up towards Blista but didn't move.

"Come on, I haven't got all day you imbecile."

Saffa still didn't move. Instead he said quietly, "No."

"What did you say?"

This time Saffa spoke louder with more confidence. "I said no. I'm not coming with you. I'd rather spend the rest of my life in prison than spend another minute with you."

Blista looked angrily at Saffa but knew he didn't have time to argue. "You'll regret this Saffa. You will all regret this!" And with that he pushed a button to close the pilot's hatch.

Chuttle reached for his proton pulse gun that was tucked into the waistband of his trousers and started firing at the JXX7.

"It's no good, the JXX7 is protected by an energy neutralising film," said Mo.

"What does that mean? asked Chuttle.

"It means you would need something the size of a shoulder canon to even make a dent," said Maffee.

"It also means that I'm getting out of here," Blista's voice came out over the JXX7's external speaker. "But I'm not finished with all of you. I'm taking this prototype back to my headquarters where I'll have a fleet of them built quicker than you can get back to Earth and go crying to your crumbly old government friends. And let's be real about this, no-one is going to believe your story anyway, you have no proof. While you're trying to persuade everyone about what happened, I'll be getting ready to take over the Earth. So, see you back on Earth, and have your mining tools ready. Ha, ha, ha," as Blista laughed, his hands moved over the controls. Suddenly, they were all blinded by a flash of white light.

They opened their eyes expecting to see the JXX7 gone, but it was still there.

"Perhaps it wasn't ready after all," said Mo and winked at Saffa.

"Right, in that case Blista, you're taking the slow route home with us, locked up in the cargo hold," Chuttle climbed the stepladder to the pilot's cockpit.

"He's not there!" said a shocked Chuttle. "He can't have slipped past us can he?"

They all looked at each other then looked around the room.

"Something must have gone wrong with the departicularisation process. Perhaps it's somehow sent Blista somewhere without moving the JXX7," said Mo.

"Gone? Just like that, flash-bish-bash. Can we find out where?" asked Chuttle.

"If the process has malfunctioned, he could be anywhere," she replied.

"Well as long as he's nowhere near us, I'm quite satisfied," said Maffee. "I don't think I could deal with anymore guards, Beasts, troopers, explosions, attacks, chases or prisons. I just want to get back to the office, my job and my mundane, happy and safe life. Can we do that now please?"

"Soon Maffee, there's a couple of things to sort out here first, then we can go home. There are a lot of workers here who have been held captive for too long. It's about time they were set free." said Mo.

Chapter Twenty Eight

Maffee was humming a tune to himself while he dusted the desktops. He tutted as he lifted up the brown coffee mug and saw the ring it had left on the desk. He pointed his right index finger at the stain and a jet of furniture polish sprayed out onto the desk and he continued to wipe.

He loved his job. He loved being back in the office, especially after the improved security measures had been put into place. His experiences of the worlds outside had made him appreciate even more the simple, quiet and safe lifestyle that he had. Back into his normal routine there were no illegal weapons dealers and car chases. There were no troopers or planetary defence units shooting at him and there were no power-crazed, insane businessmen with visions of world domination trying to throw him in a prison or enslave him in a mine for the rest of his life. With Mo working in the office again, everything was as it should be. He was looking forward to spending the rest of his days just as he wanted, cleaning, cooking and looking after his team of scientists, which now included Saffa who Mo had taken pity on and had offered him the chance to return to Earth and join the SWORD team.

Of course, Maffee was very pleased that Blista had been stopped. After Blista disappeared, Chuttle had found the communications room and called the InterEarth Government. Once the Troopers arrived, the mine was shut down and Lychee and the guards were all arrested. Blista's disappearance remained a mystery. Mo couldn't work out how he had disappeared. She had told them that it was possible that either he had been vaporised to nothing or perhaps the departicularisation had half-worked, sending him somewhere else but leaving the JXX7 where it stood. Maffee didn't care, as long as Blista was far, far away.

King Mukuto was delighted to have his planet back again and made plans to contact his people and bring them back to Suvmar, and bring Suvmar back to life. He had been very excited and couldn't thank Maffee and Chuttle enough for getting rid of Blista. He invited them both to stay on Suvmar and offered them important jobs in his new government but they had both politely turned him down. Maffee wanted to return to Earth and Chuttle seemed to have other plans as well. Unfortunately for Maffee, Chuttle had spent the whole return journey back to Earth telling him about his plans for the future. Chuttle was ready to be thrust into celebrity status. He would start by giving interviews to the World News Network. He thought that people deserved to know about how he had saved the world from certain doom by using the mental and physical skills possessed only by a great Space Detective. Once his name was as well known as McTucky Fried Jeefburgers he would announce the creation of the Chuttle Space Detective Agency. He was sure people would come to him to solve their problems and tackle wrong-doing on their behalf.

Indeed, Maffee had seen more than enough of Chuttle's large, furry head on the news. There were even rumours that Chuttle was to be nominated for the Earth's Most Valuable Being award. Maffee was sure that if Chuttle was voted as EMVB his head would get even bigger. Even Peggy was talking about Chuttle. Every time Maffee went to his shop, Peggy would make him stay and tell him about their adventure. But Maffee didn't really mind. He was secretly quite pleased that Chuttle had got what he wanted. After all, if it hadn't been for Chuttle's help, things might have turned out very differently.

The important things for Maffee were that everyone was now safely back on Earth and he was back to working in the office, where the most exciting thing to concern him was the arrival of a new floor polish at Peggy's shop.

Maffee's in-com beeped. It was Mo. "Maffee, would you come into my office please."

"Certainly Miss Draper, I'm on my way," Maffee hurried around the corridor to Mo's office. He knocked on the door and it slid open.

"Ayyyy. It's the man of the moment. Captain Courage, Admiral Action, Colonel Conqueror, my old friend Maffee. You're looking ice cool like a frozen pond my man."

Chuttle was sitting at the side of Mo's desk. He was dressed in a new silver suit with short sleeves and short trousers, pockets bulging as usual. He stood up, leapt across the office and gave Maffee a big, friendly hug.

"It's good to see you again. How's tricks you old war hero?"

"I'm not a war hero and I don't do tricks. However, I am pleased to see you again, in the flesh that is and not just on the News."

"Oh yeah. They just can't seem to get enough of the Chuttle. It's a good job there's plenty of me to go around. So what have you been up to? I bet you've been getting into more adventures without telling me. Trying to hog all the glory for yourself," Chuttle said with a smile, but Maffee didn't understand the joke.

"Certainly not. I'm back to my old job and that's where I'm staying."

"He's joking with you Maffee," said Mo.

"I've got to admit, I didn't think you would be fighting much crime with a duster in your hand. Unless it's a new secret weapon you guys have been working on," said Chuttle.

"It's the weapon of my chosen war. The war on dust!" Maffee said.

"Smoking Joseph! I don't believe it. You actually made a joke. An attempt at humour, are you sure you're not malfunctioning?"

They all smiled. This was the first time they had all met up again since returning to Earth and they were pleased to see each other again.

"Well you know what I've been doing," said Maffee waving his duster in the air. "What have you got planned next?"

"I'm glad you asked me that. That's one of the reasons I called in today. I've done enough mixing with celebrities. I feel in need of some action. So tomorrow I'm going to announce to the world that the Space Detective Agency is ready for business, ready to take on our first case. What do you think?"

"Very good. I'm very happy for you. I'm sure you'll have plenty of clients."

"Exactly. The office is all set up. You'll have your own office next door to mine. Mine's a bit larger of course, but then I need more room and I'm the Head of Space Detective Operations. But don't worry, you'll have a sign on your door too, how do you like the sound of Chief of Intelligence?"

"What?" said Maffee, confused again.

"Chief of Intelligence. You know, to reflect your brain power. If you don't like it we can change it. How about Director of Mind Operations?"

"No, no, no. I mean, what are you talking about? I have no intention of ever leaving this office again. Thanks to Miss Draper I have the job of my dreams. The Government has promised that I'll be a cleaner for the rest of my operating life."

"Hold on there. Are you serious? This is the opportunity of a lifetime. We're the most famous Space Detectives in the Universe. People will be queuing up for us to combat crime. It's going to be all action and satisfaction. You'll be rich and famous."

"If I join you on anymore of your missions, I'll also be dead! Shot to pieces by some crazy criminal, or imprisoned for life by the Dictator of a rogue planet. As tempting as that offer sounds, I think I'll stick to the hum-drum life of a cleaner, thank you!"

"What? Why wouldn't anyone want to be a Space Detective? You'll be missing out on all the action. Think of the shootouts, dog fights in space, solving crime, bringing villains to justice."

"That's exactly what I am thinking about and precisely the reason I'm more than happy not to take you up on your offer."

"But we're a team. Look at the way we rescued Miss Draper and rid the world of Gumby Gelt. With us around, no criminal would be safe."

"With you around, no-one is safe."

"Exactly!" Chuttle agreed not realising quite what Maffee meant.

"Look, I'm extremely pleased that Miss Draper is back here

178

safely and I don't know how that would have happened if I hadn't met you, but, I'm not designed for the life of a Space Detective. I don't think my systems could take the stress of danger and excitement every day, whereas you seem to have action running through your veins. So I think it is better that I stay here and leave the crime fighting in your safe hands."

Chuttle thought about this then said, "I guess you're right. But, if you change your mind, if you start to miss the taste of danger and feel the need to get back into the jungle out there, then let me know. Good partners are hard to find."

"Well I guess I'll head off then, out into the wild world and the shadows of space. Time and crime wait for no one. You folks take care and try to stay out of trouble while I'm gone."

Mo stood up and walked around her desk to Chuttle. She gave him a hug and then pulled his head down to give him a kiss on his furry cheek. "Be careful Chuttle and come back and see us soon."

"Yes be careful and don't do anything too stupid or dangerous," Maffee added.

Chuttle picked up his silver cowboy hat from the edge of Mo's desk and placed it on his head. The door slid open as he walked over to it. He stopped and turned

"One other thing Maffee," he said.

"Yes?"

"Don't spend all your time in the cupboards," Chuttle smiled as he said this, then turned and headed out of the Government building and into the world of the Space Detective.

Printed in Great Britain
by Amazon

19180229R00104